MODEEN REDEMPTION

FRANK H JORDAN

ACKNOWLEDGMENTS

The situations, organisations, and characters in this book are fictional, and any resemblance to an existing or past entity is entirely coincidental.

This book is written in Australian English.

DEDICATION

To all the readers who take the time to post thoughtful book reviews - you are appreciated more than you know

THE AUTHOR

A long time fan of Lee Child's Jack Reacher novels and Matthew Reilly's fast-paced stories, ex-Army Reservist and Queensland author Frank H Jordan penned his own high-action series inspired by the brave men and women of the Australian Defence Force.

Enter, ex-SASR soldier Jo Modeen.

Modeen Redemption is the sixth book in the thrilling **Jo Modeen** series, and follows on from *Modeen Rogue, Modeen Convergence, Modeen: Black Ops, The Modeen Transformation,* and the book that started it all, *The Modeen Factor.*
And there are plenty more adventures to come....

Connect with Frank online at *www.frankhjordanauthor. blogspot.com.au*

THE MISSION

Protect the deadly new prototype at all costs

With an unknown faction vying for control of the Black Mamba criminal organisation, it's uncertain at first who is behind an attempted hit on ex-agents Wolf and Modeen. And NatSec team leader Ben Logan has a more pressing issue on his hands. The US Department of Defence is demanding additional on-ground surveillance at a high-tech Australian laboratory, where final testing is underway of an advanced weapon, one that could alter the course of modern warfare and cement America's position as the world's dominant superpower.
Unless the prototype falls into the wrong hands....

CHAPTER ONE

The glow from the well-lit highway illuminated the burnt-out shell of the black Chrysler 300 stretch limo. It lay smouldering on its roof in a ditch, impuissant, like an upturned beetle. On the nearby south-eastern arterial highway connecting the capital city, Auckland, to the rest of New Zealand's North Island, traffic was light. In the distance the last of the Emergency Services vehicles, an ambulance, trundled off having retrieved what was left of the limo driver.

Luke Jackson watched it go and checked the time.

O-four hundred.

Skirting around the wreck, he paused every now and then to squat on his haunches and study the ground.

'Pick up any tracks, Spook?' Barry Pritchard's voice came from the other side of the wrecked vehicle.

Spooky straightened. 'As expected, there're footprints all over the place, Bugs. Those Emergency Services guys have no respect for forensics.'

'Anythin' useful?'

'There's a set of tracks heading east across the flats for about two hundred metres. They stop at the highway. I'm guessing Patel caught a ride from there.'

Bugs made his way around the limo, pushing through patches of tall grass that left damp marks on the legs of his dark-coloured cargo pants. He shivered in the brisk air. The sun wouldn't be up for another two hours.

'Looks like he dragged himself three quarters of the way,' Spooky went on as Bugs joined him. 'Then two guys came down off the shoulder there,' and he pointed to the road, 'to carry him back up to the highway. From the wayward direction of the tracks, I'm guessing he must've been hurt pretty bad in the crash.'

'He was lucky to've even *survived* it if y'ask me,' Bugs said drily.

———

In the waning glow of late evening, a US Air Force C17 Globemaster appeared on the eastern horizon. It was on approach to Woomera military facility, the largest land-based test facility in the southern hemisphere, located five hundred kilometres north-east of Adelaide and encompassing over a hundred and twenty-two thousand square kilometres of South Australia's Great Victoria Desert.

The airborne leviathan's landing lights blazed on as twelve huge wheels lowered from its undercarriage. They took the brunt of the cargo plane's massive weight as it touched down and taxied to a stop. Ground crew scurried to secure the aircraft, whose rear cargo ramp was already being lowered. A short time later an eight-wheeled military vehicle nosed its way down the ramp and was escorted inside the facility's main hangar.

At o-six hundred the following morning Philip Morris and two defence force technicians drove the vehicle, an all-terrain Oshkosh truck, out of the hangar and exited the compound. After travelling for two hours they came to a stop near a rocky outcrop in the middle of the desert. It offered commanding views of the surrounding landscape, where hectares of low spinifex grass and acacia bushes, the only vegetation capable of surviving the harsh environment, stretched for kilometres.

The three men weren't there to take in the views. Stretching as they exited the transport, they eyed the bulky turret mounted on the vehicle's roof. The Oshkosh was the ideal mobile platform to test the joint military project's latest and most powerful acquisition, a three hundred and forty kilowatt multiple-fibre pulse laser.

When Morris and his team had finished making the final adjustments to the high-energy weapon, they climbed down from the truck's roof to pile into the cabin, where Morris turned on the targeting computer. The centre console-mounted touch screen blinked into life with the Department of Defence's logo, followed by a glowing green radar screen. Its indicator arm passed over the circle's radius in continual sweeps as the words *Acquiring target* in bold text appeared in the centre. Using the on-screen menu, Morris switched the targeting option to Manual, and the display changed to a real-time image of the range, projected from the camera also mounted on the truck's roof.

He zoomed in on the target, located ten kilometres to the north-west of their location. The M113AS1 personnel carrier sat forlornly in front of a low ridge that stretched for kilometres either side of it. A relic of the Vietnam war, the broken-down armour-plated transport looked more like a tank. Too badly damaged to warrant repairs and the upgrades necessary to meet the current S4 standard, it sat lopsided, missing one of its tracks. Inside, two forty-four gallon drums of black powder were its only cargo.

Morris glanced down at the screen and watched the laser's power bar rise incrementally as he guided the crosshairs onto the target. When they flashed green, he tapped on the comms unit in his left ear. 'Woomera Base, this is FR3. We are good to go.'

A reply came back immediately. 'Roger, FR3. Airspace has been closed. Taipan One, report.'

There was a crackle over the comms, and a moment later the pilot of the MRH90 helicopter hovering at five thousand feet above and to the left behind the Oshkosh announced, 'This is Taipan One. Confirm range and airspace are clear.'

'Roger, Taipan One. FR3, this is Woomera Base. You are OK to go. Fire when ready.'

'Roger, Woomera Base.'

Woop, woop, woop.

As the audible warning alarm issued from the comms, Morris gave the two techs a cursory glance. At their nods, he tapped his index finger on the FIRE button icon.

Inside the truck's cabin, the only sound came from the air-conditioning unit as it pumped artificially cooled air over its occupants. They sat with eyes fixed on the touch screen's display, hardly breathing. While there was no tangible indication that anything had happened, on the screen a mushroom cloud formed where the personnel carrier had been. Twenty-nine seconds later they heard a faint boom in the distance as the blast wave buffeted the Oshkosh.

• • •

Returning to base later that day, Morris and the technicians collected the video recordings and data taken from the remote camera feeds and sensors set up to monitor the test. They hurried to the lab to view the recordings, and watched a white-hot glow appear on the front of the target a split second before the laser beam melted through the quarter-inch armour plating, igniting the black powder which disintegrated the vehicle.

Morris sat back in his seat, still staring at the monitor. 'Well, that's it for the laser test on a static target,' he announced. Lifting his head, he nodded at the techs. 'Stage two, upgrade the platform and activate the radar targeting system.'

The techs whooped and high-fived, and one of them exclaimed, 'Celebratory drinks tonight!' When he didn't get the expected animated response from Morris he frowned. 'You'll be in that won't ya, Phil?'

Morris didn't reply.

———

Off Fairlie Road near Lake Tekapo in New Zealand's south island, a black Lada SUV pulled up next to a set of wide, double-padlocked gates. Beyond them a track meandered up the side of a snow-capped mountain toward an abandoned ski field. The two men gazed through the SUV's windscreen at the old, two storey lodge positioned on a ridge halfway up the mountain.

Smoke was just visible, billowing from its two chimneys.

The older of the two men nodded to his comrade as he opened the driver's door. Freezing air swept into the warm cabin, but neither man gave any indication of being chilled. They set off, trudging along the snow-swathed track, their heavy boots leaving twin muddy ditches in their wake. They passed torn, twisted sections of dual-seat chairlift sticking out of the snow in places. An avalanche some years before had thrown the ski field's top wheelhouse off the mountain, like a giant shrugging off a biting insect, leaving its shattered remains scattered down the slope below.

On the lodge's balcony a pair of eyes watched the two men approach. Lowering the binoculars, the guard hurried inside to announce, 'We've got company, boss. Two men walking up the track, Ruskies I reckon. It'll take 'em about ten minutes to get here.'

When his boss raised his head and frowned, the messenger hastily looked away from the mutilated visage of dreadlocks seared back to the skull, above puckered facial skin covered in raw and weeping pustules. What remained of the man's left eyelid was blistered and inflamed over an opaque, glazed eye that was once an icy blue.

Rubbing his good eye, the boss opened his laptop and followed their visitors' progress on the screen, projected there by CCTV cameras positioned along the route.

. . .

The two men were ushered into the boss's office accompanied by three of his goons, all hefty Islanders, who filed in behind them to position themselves, arms folded, against the rear wall. Sitting back in his chair, the boss took in his visitors' full length, wool-lined leather coats. The front brims of their Cossack-style fur hats were pushed up vertically, both displaying a white hammer and sickle symbol against a red star. Hanks of greasy blonde hair issued from beneath the hat of the taller Russian, whose other most noticeable feature was the concave bridge and flattened tip of his large, spider-veined nose. His comrade was thinner, wiry, with features more Asian than Russian.

The man with the boxer's nose gave a loud sniff and stepped forward, smirking at the grotesque scarring on the side of the boss man's face. In a guttural, heavily accented voice he announced, 'Ze Bratva are not happy … Patel.'

Owen Patel eyed him and sneered through blistered lips, 'The who?'

The Russian's expression didn't change. 'Ve represent ze brotherhood,' he continued evenly, 'and ze brotherhood is not happy vis your progress.'

Glaring daggers at him from his one working eye, Patel snapped, 'And why should I give a *crap* what you or your brotherhood thinks?'

The Russian leaned forward to rest meaty hands on

the desk, gold rings glinting on each finger. Smirking into Patel's grotesque face he said in a tone slick with self-assurance, 'Tell me, do you actually believe you are in control?'

The man's stale breath and undisguised air of contempt had Patel leaping to his feet. With a roar of, 'Enough!' he thumped the desk with a fist. 'I am Nakahi Pango, the Black Mamba, and you will show me some *respect.*'

The Russian narrowed his eyes and puffed out his cheeks. He released the air through his thick lips with a pop, and then gave a grunt. Taking this as capitulation, Patel visibly relaxed. The Russian straightened, slipping a hand beneath his jacket as though reaching for a cigarette … only to withdraw it an instant later gripping a Lebedev nine millimetre pistol.

Patel had enough time to suck in a breath and widen his good eye before the Russian levelled the gun and fired. At such close range, the bullet tore through Patel's right clavicle and into the wall behind him, a spray of crimson accompanying it.

As their boss dropped to the floor with an agonised yell, two of his goons leapt forward, reaching for their weapons, only to clutch at their throats as blue titanium knives dug deep into each of their larynxes. Gagging, they dropped to their knees and collapsed to the floor. Across the room the shorter of the two Russians came to a spinning stop, both hands empty after completing the throws.

He side-stepped smoothly when the third goon darted forward, pivoting anti-clockwise as he did so and slipping another throwing knife from a scabbard strapped to his right thigh. As the thick-set goon pounded past him, grabbing at air, the light-footed Russian completed his graceful three-sixty degree turn and drove the blade into the back of the Islander's neck.

With a satisfied grunt, the man with the boxer's nose moved around the desk to eye Patel, who was lying on the floor propped on one elbow. Breathing heavily, Patel stared up at his attacker in disbelief, one hand pressed to his shoulder to stem the bleeding.

'I am Vladimir Debeljah,' the Russian said matter-of-factly, once more aiming the pistol, this time at Patel's forehead. 'And *zis* is for not taking better care of my *leettle* brother, Sergio.' He paused to let that sink in, clearly savouring Patel's open-mouthed look of terror, before slowly squeezing the trigger.

CHAPTER TWO

At the rap of knuckles on his office door, Ben Logan raised his head to see NatSec's Operations Manager Jack Pender stride in. Closing the file he'd been perusing, Ben sat back in his chair and returned his boss's nod of greeting.

'I've read your brief on the New Zealand event,' Jack announced. 'Beta team and Ms Bennet were lucky that things ended in our favour.'

Ben watched him take a seat in front of the desk and frowned. 'But we didn't get Patel.'

'Yes.' Jack pursed his lips. 'That was a missed opportunity.'

'I agree.' Ben leaned forward, resting his arms on the desk. 'And I believe it would be in the agency's best interest to pursue the Black Mambas and shut down their operations.' When Jack merely raised his eyebrows in an unspoken, 'Go on,' Ben continued.

'They're a fanatical group of thugs, Jack. If left unchecked they'll only grow in numbers. Owen Patel is still on the loose, and from what JD learned there's a bounty on the head of each member of my team.' He paused to eye his boss before plunging on. 'Three weeks, that's all I'd need to tie up the loose ends.'

Jack shook his head and said brusquely, 'Negative.' He sat forward. 'Look Ben, I take your point, but Patel's probably going to lay low for a while, licking his wounds. And I'm betting he'll have his hands full defending the Mambas' territory now the newly elected Queensland Government has repealed the Lawlessness Act. Sure as anything, the previously outlawed motor-cycle gangs will return to reclaim their old territories.' He gave a satisfied nod. 'Patel will be too busy dealing with all that to worry about coming after your team. And anyway, we have more pressing priorities.'

Ben ran a hand through his hair and leaned back, the chair creaking beneath his six foot four, well-muscled frame. 'Well,' he sighed, 'I can't say I'm not disappointed.'

'Don't be. You'll get another chance if the Mambas cross paths with us again.' Jack gave a wry snort and sat back in his seat. 'Unless the bikers beat us to them, of course.'

Pushing Patel to the back of his mind, Ben said, 'So, do any of those "pressing priorities" involve my team?'

'Yes, and this one's come out of left field.' Jack

threw him a meaningful glance as he rose to shut the door. Resuming his seat, he rubbed his hands together. 'I've been contacted by my counterpart in the US who's been working closely with the CIA in Langley, Virginia, on a highly confidential case. They have reason to believe that information on a classified military project is being leaked, and suspect one of the project engineers may be the source of the leak.'

Ben frowned. 'Sounds like something the Yanks'd want to handle in-house. Why would they be involving NatSec?'

'I'll send through all the details when I receive them, but what I can tell you now is that the engineer in question, one Philip Morris, is Australian. He works for Advanced Laser Optics, a major US defence contractor, and is a key member of the project team. ALO is based in Nowra but Morris has been flying between there and the US over the last eighteen months. We've been requested to keep him under surveillance while he's here in Oz.'

'I see.' Curiosity glinted in Ben's eyes. 'What do we know about the project he's working on?'

'It's quite exciting really.' Enthusiasm radiated from Jack's face and voice. 'The US Air Force is in the final stages of putting together a prototype sixth-generation jet fighter to replace the F-22 Raptor. A successful result will ensure they maintain air superiority, hence the need for secrecy.'

'They're replacing the Raptor? Didn't they develop the F-35 Lightning for that purpose?'

'No, it was designed to replace the Falcon, Hornet and Thunderbolt, and intended to complement the Raptor. That's why the Lightning's offered in three variants. Being smaller, it can be launched from an aircraft carrier, but with only one engine it can't super-cruise like the Raptor. It's horses for courses.'

'So we're talking about a whole new aircraft design?'

Jack rubbed his chin. 'They're not overly forth-coming with specifics ... but from what I can gather, the Raptor's superior stealth capability is the reason American federal law banned its export. Although its limited agility hampers it in close-quarter dogfights it's still a formidable fighter, so I'm guessing the design modifications will encompass some airframe ameliora-tion but focus primarily on weaponry and counter-measures.'

'I see.' Ben nodded. 'When I was enlisted, the Yanks were known to be working on laser technology. I believe the US Navy had even successfully tested a direct energy weapon in the field.'

'Yes,' Jack said briskly, 'and not just lasers. They're also developing EMP and electromagnetic projectile launchers. The Raptor is limited to the amount and type of long-range missiles it can carry while still main-taining its stealth profile, but imagine what it would be like if it were fitted with laser or EMP weapons ... or both. For a start it wouldn't have to worry about manoeuvrability, it could sneak up on enemy planes, deploy the EMP and knock out their on-board computers. Any fly-by-wire aircraft, and that's almost all modern planes and choppers, would just fall out of the sky.'

Ben eyed him with mild amusement. 'You're really into all this aren't you?'

Jack gave a wry grin. 'I haven't always been a desk jockey, you know. I used to fly Hueys out of Phuoc Tuyat back in Vietnam.'

Ben returned the grin. 'You're a man of many talents, Jack.'

———

At a roadside café on Lygon Street in Melbourne's restaurant precinct, Troy Wolverton took a long sip of his coffee and gazed across the table at his platinum-blonde companion. 'We've been back from New Zealand a week now,' he drawled. 'I think we're temptin' fate stayin' in your Gold Coast apartment. We know it's been compromised.'

Josephine Dakota Modeen nodded and set down her cup. 'Yeah, and I've multi-listed it with some real estate agents already, but it's not going to sell overnight.'

'You're gonna miss that penthouse aren't you?'

'I guess so.' She looked thoughtful. 'And not just

me. Aunty Hannah and Salty have been regular visitors lately. But now I wouldn't feel comfortable about leaving them there on their own.'

Wolf gave an amused huff. 'Don't underestimate Salty, he's one capable old fart.'

'I know, but if anything were to happen to either of them....'

He sat back, regarding her intently for a long moment, before straightening and leaning forward. 'So, why don't we get a place of our own, you and me?'

She widened her china blue eyes at him. 'You mean … move in together?' and was awarded with one of his crooked grins.

'Sure. We could always stay at my place in Canberra, at least until we decide on our next move.'

'Don't you mean Bugs' place?' She raised a teasing eyebrow at him.

'Humph! NatSec might subsidise the rent but it's still *my* name on the lease, so Bugs is still officially my guest.' Wolf sobered. 'Don't get me wrong, I'm glad he moved in and kept an eye on the place while I was … out of action.' He cleared his throat. 'He can always take over the lease when we go. Besides, there's plenty of room and he's hardly ever there anyway.'

Modeen chewed her lip. 'I don't fancy staying in Canberra for long, the winters there are just too damn cold.' She sat back in her seat and regarded him thoughtfully. 'Are you sure that's what you want, Troy?'

He didn't hesitate. 'I'm sure. Like I said, we can drop off the radar. And if the Black Mamba or anyone else with a grudge ever comes a-knockin', they'll be sorry.' Throwing her a confident wink he rocked back in his chair and linked his fingers behind his head, a recently shaved patch still visible in his dark hair.

Modeen's smile froze on her lips and the blood drained from her face as a red dot suddenly shimmered on the circular table between them. With a yell of, 'Down!' she thrust the table at Wolf while diving for cover herself.

As he fell backwards, limbs flailing, Wolf's size eleven boots launched the metal table into the air, sending its contents flying. At the same time a spark and a loud metallic ricochet had the patrons around them flinching and ducking for cover.

After landing on his back Wolf twisted around, searching for Modeen. Seeing her lying flat on the ground against the maroon canvas partition that delineated the dining area from the street, he scrambled onto his hands and knees and zigzagged between the tables and chairs, flinging himself down beside her. 'You alright?'

She nodded. 'You?'

'Fine, thanks to your quick thinkin'.'

Her expression softened for an instant and then she was all business again. 'The shot came from up high and to the south-west, diagonally across the Lygon-

Queensberry intersection. The big red brick building,' and she indicated it with a lift of her chin.

Raising his head for a quick glimpse over the partition, Wolf lowered it again with a nod of agreement.

On the other side of the partition, a City Transit bus rumbled up to the four-way intersection and came to a jerking stop at the traffic lights with a hiss of air brakes. Modeen peeked over the partition at it and then turned to Wolf. 'You take this side of the street. I'll cross over from here, I've got cover.'

Rising to his haunches, Wolf sprang forward and sprinted across the footpath, trying not to bowl over any bewildered patrons on the way. Behind him, sparks ricocheted off the pavement as another two shots rang out. Launching himself into the café's doorway, he slid to a stop. From there he peered across the intersection at the red brick building, and then gave Modeen the signal to go.

She leapt up and, using the bus for cover, vaulted over the partition. Circling around the back of the City Transit, she paused to time the oncoming traffic before dashing across the two double lanes. Once on the other side of the road she flattened herself against a wall under a wide shop awning close to the corner.

Across the intersection the four storey, red-brick building jutted above the rooflines of its neighbouring shops. Modeen eyed the top balconies. Their dark-tinted windows all faced Queensberry Street, and there was no sign of movement. She scanned the roofline and glimpsed the back of a man's head as he disappeared from view, heading toward the centre of the roof.

Turning, she signalled Wolf to advance. He took a precautionary glance down the street as he left cover, darting out to run to the corner and then across the intersection on his side of the road. Coming to a stop, he flattened himself against the wall of the "Down Towner" building. He scanned the red brick building opposite, searching for any movement. With no windows on that side of the structure, the building looked even more imposing. Its footprint stretched sixty metres down Lygon Street from the corner, ending in an atrium separating it from what appeared to be a different section of the same building at the rear.

Using hand motions, Wolf signalled for Modeen to cover the front of the building while he entered through the side. He watched her run diagonally across the road to where a high fence in the same dark red brick led up a flight of stairs to the building's main entrance. Making his way down Lygon Street he crossed the road and passed the atrium, which was also sectioned off by a low wall of the same-coloured brick. After striding up a wide access ramp that doubled back to a set of heavy glass doors, he slipped inside the building.

Mounted high on the wall at one end of the small entry foyer, a glossy board displayed the businesses located on each floor of that section of the building. To Wolf's right, a wide corridor led to the local member's office, a solicitor's firm, and another set of double glass doors that opened onto the atrium. The door to his left, displaying an amenities decal, had an emergency exit sign directly above it.

Wolf went through the exit door and found himself in a long, narrow passageway. The bright glow of the fluorescent lights running down the centre of the ceiling reflected off the white paintwork. Small storage rooms were situated along the left of the corridor. On the right, doors leading to the male and female amenities were separated by a janitor's storeroom. Jogging the full length of the passageway, he came to another exit door at the far end and burst through it.

At the big man's sudden appearance in the small lane at the side of the building, two beefy Islanders and an Asian man leaning against a Chrysler sedan gave a start, and whirled around to face him.

CHAPTER THREE

Slipping through the front door, Modeen scanned the building's interior. Once part of the Royal Melbourne Institute of Technology's campus, which encompassed several neighbouring buildings, it retained a quiet aura of academia. There was even a lingering smell of textbooks on the air. This was despite the building having been on-sold by the university as part of an asset liquidation programme, to be subsequently turned into a shopping gallery-come office block by its new owners.

Glancing toward the stainless steel doors of the two large elevators – large enough to accommodate laden library trolleys, photocopiers and other scholastic equipment – Modeen ran her eyes over the tenant listing on the corporate board mounted on the wall between the lifts. Her ears caught laughter coming from the back left corner of the expansive foyer, where a busy Coffee Club franchise spilled into the adjacent atrium. To the café's right, a jewellery shop and hair salon flanked an evening wear boutique, where downlights sparkled off flowing, sequined creations displayed on waif-like mannequins.

When the left elevator pinged, she watched a corporate couple exit and make for the Coffee Club.

The alley.

She retraced her steps to the front entrance, took a final look behind, and then raced down the stairs and veered left. Slowing to a jog she swerved left again and ducked down the narrow laneway running alongside the building. From the dumpsters positioned side-by-side next to the main loading dock, it appeared the alleyway was mainly used by delivery and waste removal vehicles.

Spying the front fender and bonnet of a dark blue Chrysler sedan jutting out at the end of the lane, Modeen quickened her pace. She gave the vehicle a wide berth as she turned the corner, in time to see Wolf suddenly duck his head. With a flash of blue, two titanium throwing knives whistled past his ears and lodged themselves with resonating thuds into the open door behind him.

She glimpsed another flash of blue as an Asian man raised his arm, a third knife in his hand. Leaping onto the bonnet and then the roof of the Chrysler, she launched herself at the man, letting out a *Kiai* as she did so. The marital arts attacking scream had the desired effect. The Asian turned his head to receive the full force of her combat boot to the side of this face. The impact sent him careering backward and to the concrete, while Modeen recoiled and landed on her feet in the spot he had just vacated. As she regained her balance and straightened, the two islanders came at her, tattooed arms extended and their meaty hands claw-like.

Yanking one of the throwing knives from the door, Wolf was about to weigh into the fracas when a tall blonde man with a misshapen nose burst through the doorway to Wolf's left. He carried a backpack over his shoulder and held a Lebedev pistol in one hand. Seeing him level the gun at Modeen, Wolf stepped forward, thrusting the knife into the man's gun hand and sweeping his leading leg as he did so. Wolf felt the blade glance off the bone just above the wrist as, with an agonised wail, the man dropped the pistol and fell backward, onto the concrete.

Police sirens could be heard squawking toward them down Queensberry Street as Wolf bent to retrieve the Lebedev, only to have his feet swept out from under him and the pistol sent sliding across the concrete. He crashed to the ground next to the blonde man, who stomped the heel of his boot into Wolf's forehead when he made to get up.

Modeen had her hands full with the two Islanders. They jostled for position, intent on trapping her between them. When one advanced, reaching for her throat, she intercepted his hand and bent his palm backward, forcing him to roll his shoulder forward and double over. The second Islander made to move in but hesitated as the sirens drew closer. He shifted his feet nervously, uncertain whether fight or flight was called for, but was left in no doubt when the knife-wielding Asian and the blonde man raced past him. As the three of them ran to the Chrysler, the blonde man yanked the knife from his arm to fling it back-handed at Modeen.

When she ducked to let the knife sail harmlessly over her head, Modeen felt her captive try to free his hand from her grip. Immediately increasing the pressure on the Islander's arm, she followed up with a couple of snap kicks to his mid-section for good measure. His body convulsed as the sharp blows hit their mark, and when she delivered a more powerful kick to his forehead, his head snapped back and he slumped to the ground.

Releasing her hold on the unconscious man, Modeen sprang toward the departing Chrysler. She managed to touch a fingertip to its boot as it tore off with a squeal of rubber and a raised middle finger from the Islander struggling to steady himself in the back seat. Tyres smoking, it took the first exit left onto Cardigan Street … and was gone. Modeen slid to a stop and bent to catch her breath as a police car appeared at the top of the lane.

Wolf walked up to put a hand on her back. 'You OK?'

'Yeah.' Seeing him rub his head, she frowned. 'What about you?'

Growling, 'I've been better,' he went on. 'I didn't recognise the other two, but the Islanders certainly looked like Mambas.' He glanced at the man spread-eagled on the ground behind them and then at the police car powering down the lane toward them. 'It's a pity we won't get a chance to interrogate him here.'

As the patrol car screeched to a halt in front of them, siren wailing and red and blue lights flashing, Modeen rolled her eyes at Wolf. 'Great, that's all we need.'

'Hold it right there!' a voice commanded as the car's doors opened and a pistol was aimed at them. 'Get down on the ground, hands behind your backs.' The senior officer and his offsider slid from their seats to crouch behind the patrol car's doors.

Leaning toward Wolf, Modeen murmured, 'You'd better give Ben a call when you get a chance.'

He nodded and then saw her expression change when she looked over her shoulder. 'What?' Following her gaze, he saw the space behind them now empty. The Islander had given them the slip. Wolf gave an exasperated shake of his head and snarled, 'Well … that's just *perfect*.'

'On the ground,' the police officer bellowed again, 'NOW!'

Wolf pointed to the open doorway. 'The guy you *should* to be chasin' just went that way.'

'I won't tell you again! On the floor NOW, with your hands behind your backs.'

Sighing, Modeen got to her knees. 'Come on Troy, we'll catch up with those guys later.' She lowered herself face down on the ground and put her hands behind her back.

A scowling Wolf followed suit, swearing under his breath. It was only when he was on the ground that the two policemen broke cover. They approached cautiously, arms outstretched, holding their nine millimetre Glocks trained on the two prone detainees.

———

Ben nosed the black NatSec Aurion sedan into a park in front of the Fitzroy Police Station. He turned off the ignition and sat back to study the seventies-styled, two storey building, idly contemplating the contrast it made with the graceful architecture of the heritage-listed library it backed onto. The drab, rectangular police station looked more like a seedy motel in a sleazy part of the outer suburbs. Its low, flat roof and window-mounted air-conditioning units, reinforced by security bars, did little for the building's aesthetics.

Ben reached for the door handle just as Wolf and Modeen came down the stairs and walked up to the car. He sat back and rolled down the window, throwing them a sideways smirk. 'I was beginning to wonder where you'd got to.'

His smirk dissolved, however, at Wolf's urgent, 'Take us back to the lane alongside the shopping gallery, off Queensberry Street.' Strapping himself into the front passenger's seat, Wolf said tersely, 'I think the Black Mambas have recruited some new players.'

With a nod of greeting to Modeen in the back seat, Ben accelerated away from the police station and turned onto Napier Street. 'That was pretty brazen of them to take a shot at you in broad daylight,' he muttered, 'it's unfortunate they got away.' At Wolf's aggravated grunt, Ben shot him a warning glance. 'We'll go back there for a look, but you need to know … the Mambas aren't NatSec's top priority at this point.'

As Ben turned into the lane between the shopping gallery and the cluster of RMIT buildings, Wolf pointed to the end of the laneway. 'Down there.' The Aurion was still coming to a stop as he leapt out and began searching the area next to one of the dumpsters.

Ben and Modeen watched him squat and reach his full arm's length beneath two of the foul-smelling bins, sweeping his hand over the concrete, before sitting back on his haunches. With a quick wipe of his hand on his pants leg he rose and returned to the car, holding a pistol between a thumb and forefinger, and wearing a satisfied grin. 'I knew the cops'd miss it,' he drawled. 'Don't like gettin' their hands dirty.'

Reaching into the glove box, Ben took out a plastic bag. He opened it and held it out. When Wolf dropped the weapon into it, Ben stared at it and murmured, 'That's a Russian PL-15 Lebedev.'

'Yeah,' Wolf said, climbing in beside him. 'And there should be some decent prints on it.'

Putting the bagged gun into the glove box, Ben raised an eyebrow at him. 'Sounds like you want to pursue this?'

Wolf frowned back at him. 'Of course we wanna pursue it. What sort of question is that?'

'Just…' Ben shrugged. 'I thought you were going to resign, Wolf, and the two of you were planning to drop off the radar?'

'That's right, we are,' Modeen interjected from the back seat. 'But being shot at when all you're doing is kicking back enjoying a coffee, kinda makes you want to know who's doing the shooting,' she said drily.

Eyeing her through the rear view mirror, Ben said, 'So…?'

'So … I got number plate details you could run, which might also provide a lead.'

'You know, if you came back to NatSec, you'd be able to run all the prints and number plates you want.' As he spoke, Ben fixed his eyes on the road again. 'And I have a low-risk surveillance job that'd be perfect for the two of you.'

Wolf turned to lock eyes with Modeen. Nobody spoke for a long moment, and then she said, 'This morning only reinforces our decision to drop off the radar, Ben. I was just hoping that if we got a lead on those responsible we could put a stop to them before Wolf and I go to ground. It'd save us from having to constantly look over our shoulders down the track.' Sighing, she muttered, 'I'm just kicking myself they got away.'

'I'm sure you did all you could in the circumstances.'

'But it wasn't enough, Ben,' she said darkly while turning to look out the window, 'and that's what matters.'

All three were silent and then Ben asked hopefully, 'What about some freelance work? Just 'til you decide where to from here.'

When Modeen didn't respond, Wolf said, 'We've already decided what we're gonna do.'

'Oh yeah, what?'

'We're gonna spend the next week in Canberra, then Bugs can take over my apartment … assumin' you still want him based there.'

'I'm sure Bugs'll be happy about that. So what's on the agenda for you two?'

'We're headin' up north.'

'Not south to Tassie?'

Wolf gave a humourless grunt. 'Nah. Spent enough time there recently.'

'Are you both *sure* you won't reconsider staying with NatSec?' Glimpsing their set expressions, Ben said firmly, 'We've made ourselves some powerful enemies, as you know, and staying with NatSec brings us a certain amount of security. I don't believe any of us will be rid of the threat of retribution, no matter where we go or what we do. Not for a *long* time at least.'

With a quick glance at Modeen, who dipped her head, Wolf said just as firmly, 'Point taken, Ben, but Jo and I really want to give this a try.'

Ben lifted his hands from the steering wheel in a brief gesture of surrender. 'Fair enough.' He gave a resigned sigh. 'Well then, I'll run the prints and number plate when we get back to HQ and let you know what we find.'

'Speakin' of prints,' Wolf growled, 'they took ours at the police station, along with a coupl'a mug shots.'

'Don't worry,' Ben said evenly, 'Leanne's got that covered.'

Back at Fitzroy Police Station, a constable at a computer gave a start as the screen in front of him, which had been displaying newly entered ID profiles of one Troy Ryan and Josephine Modeen, suddenly flashed and went blank. He rebooted the machine and typed in a search for the two latest entries, only to be confronted by the message … *No matching records found.*

CHAPTER FOUR

South of Nowra in New South Wales, Albatross Aviation Technology Park had come alive with activity following a sizeable delivery by a US Air Force C17 Globemaster. Situated beside the HMAS Albatross's airfield on the Royal Australian Naval Base and with direct runway access, AATP provided support for defence and aviation operations. It also hosted the Advanced Laser Optics laboratory which was in semi lock-down, its security having been ramped up, along with the rest of the compound, for that morning's delivery.

Inside the lab, Philip Morris stood with arms folded watching the large roller door descend behind the newly delivered crate with a rattle of chains and groan of metal. As the door thudded to a tight close against the concrete floor, shutting out the sounds of the busy military base and, more importantly, any curious eyes, he turned and barked at the lab assistant working part way down the length of the building, 'Hey, Luke! You got a forklift ticket?'

The lab assistant straightened and dusted off his hands. 'Sure do.'

'Good. Pick up this crate, take it over there,' and Morris pointed to the floor in the centre of the building, 'and open 'er up.'

'Right-o.' The lab assistant walked up to run a hand over the reinforced plywood crate, checking its structure. Stamped '160kg', the box was one and a half metres tall, one and a half metres wide and almost two and a half metres long. At his muttered, 'Whatever's in here can't weigh much,' Morris said curtly, 'Just get it done.'

With a dip of his head, the lab assistant sprang nimbly onto the waiting electric forklift, clicked the seatbelt across his waist, and raised the forklift tynes.

Morris watched him deftly manoeuvre the forklift into place as a voice behind him said, 'What's the story with that bloke, Phil?' Turning, he saw his head technician come to stand beside him.

'New lab assistant.'

The senior tech shook his head. 'More bureaucratic bullshit,' he muttered sourly. 'Who thought it was a good idea to add a new staff member at this stage of the project? Right when we're on the verge of fitting the most powerful laser on the planet to a—'

'Stop right there!' Morris thrust up a hand.

Narrowing his eyes, he leaned in to say in a low voice that held a distinct thread of tension, 'What it's being fitted to is still top secret. So keep your voice down when we talk about it, even here in the lab.' He paused to stare at the other man for a long, pensive moment. 'For that matter, have you mentioned it to anyone outside of here?'

'Of course not,' the tech blustered, 'I know the rules.'

'Not even your wife? She must be curious about what you do?'

'Not even her.'

Seeing him lower his gaze as he spoke, Morris frowned and stabbed a finger into his chest. 'This is a Level Five Security project, Brent, don't ever forget that. We're here to do the science, and that's as far as it goes for us. We don't discuss what we do with anyone and we don't ask questions. Not if we know what's good for us and our families.' At his colleague's offended expression, Morris sighed and dragged a hand through his hair. 'Look, Brent,' he said more calmly, 'this bloke,' and he lifted his chin at the lab assistant on the forklift, 'is some gifted undergrad from the New South Wales University of Innovation, here on prac placement for his Creative Intelligence degree.'

Brent gave a bemused frown. 'His *what* degree?'

'Creative intelligence. It's meant to encompass high-level critical and creative thinking.'

'Creative thinking?' Brent grunted. 'What focus

would a qualification like that have, or what field would it be in? Surely not the authentic sciences. Sounds like he should be writing science fiction, not working in a scientific lab.'

'Well,' Morris said flatly, 'I wouldn't bother asking him to explain if you don't want to be hit with buzz-words like "globalised real-world projects", "untapped strategic opportunities" and "trans-disciplinary modernisation".'

'What a load of crock!' Brent gave a bark of derisive laughter.

'All I know is that his placement was not nego-tiable, and was authorised at the highest level of government, so it wasn't like I could say no. And we all know what these military projects are like, hangers-on like this come with the territory.'

Watching the lab assistant raise the tynes slowly having secured the load, Brent ran his eyes over the younger man. Taking in his pushed-up fringe, neat clothing and tanned, muscular arms, he mused, 'For a uni student he's pretty buff … doesn't strike me as someone who spends his waking hours hunched over textbooks, and the rest of the time partying with his mates. And he'd have to be in his late twenty's … a bit old for your average uni student, isn't it?'

Morris said resignedly, 'Like I said, his clearance came from the highest level, so I assume his placement here was sanctioned by the Defence Department.' When Brent made as if to speak again, Morris said firmly, 'We just need to tread carefully and watch what we say around him.' Frowning, he turned away muttering to himself, 'Especially if he's here to keep an eye on us.'

With smooth, decisive movements the crate was lowered to the concrete floor in the centre of the expansive lab building. After getting a thumbs-up from Morris, the assistant backed the forklift to clear the tynes from the base of the pallet, and then returned the forklift to its docking station. Moments later he jogged back via the storeroom carrying a crowbar, which he used to jimmy the top off the crate.

'Luke,' Morris called, tilting his head toward the man standing beside him, 'this is Brent, my senior technician.' As the two men shook hands he went on. 'Whenever I'm not here, Brent's in charge, and what he says goes.'

With an amiable nod at them, Luke returned to the crate to drop down the side panels. After stacking them against the wall, he came back to stand with the other two men and the three of them studied the contents of the crate.

The highly-polished silver-grey titanium composite frame gleamed up at them from its bed of packing material. It looked space-age in design. A thick wiring harness stretched from the front to the back of the frame and was neatly secured to it with stainless steel clips.

Nudging Brent with an elbow, Morris turned to Luke. 'Well, Mr Creative Intelligence, what do you make of this?'

Ignoring the jibe, Luke peered down at the frame and said thoughtfully, 'Well .. the top panel's stamped *Lockheed – Fort Worth, Texas, Air Force plant 4*, so I'm guessing this is part of an airframe.' He rubbed his fashionably stubbled chin. 'Given its size, I'd say … from a US fighter plane maybe?'

Morris gave an approving nod. 'Not a bad guess. But what it was made for is of no consequence as it's to be fitted to something else entirely.' He tossed Luke a set of keys. 'And that "something" is parked in shed number two, out the back. Be a good lad and get it for us.'

———

'Report.' As usual, Ben was all business.

'Morris is an older bloke, weedy and gruff, hardly ever cracks a smile. Strikes me as the usual egg-head scientist type. I haven't seen anything to indicate he's up to no good. He and his Two-IC start work at o-seven hundred and finish at twenty hundred hours, and as far as I can tell they don't socialise much.'

With a grunt of acknowledgement, Ben enquired, 'So what've they had you doing, Spook?'

'Well, we've stripped down a laser turret from the roof of an Oshkosh troop carrier, and are retro-fitting it to an airframe that was shipped in yesterday from Lockheed, Fort Worth. I've secured the lab's video footage from last night and will send it through ASAP.'

'Good work. So they've swallowed your cover story?'

'Yeah, but I've caught Morris looking at me sideways a few times so I wouldn't say he's entirely convinced. Have managed to side-step his trickier questions by reciting some of the nerdy waffle from that uni blurb you sent me … seems to have worked so far. By the way, did you make that stuff up?'

Ben gave an amused huff. 'No, that's an actual degree offered by the Uni.'

'Yeah? Could'a fooled me. Anyway, while I was ripping out fibre optic conduits, drilling holes and re-routing the cables to new control panels on the airframe, I was thinking how this assignment would've been perfect for Modeen. She used to like playing with this sort of tech stuff in the Force, and she was good at it.'

'Yeah, I know,' Ben sighed, 'and if it were up to me I would've had her on the job in a heartbeat. But I've got to respect her decision to leave the agency. Hers and Wolf's.' He paused before going on more firmly. 'On another note, I've had Bugs on surveillance of Morris's house. He's reported seeing no sign of the wife, Susan, to this point. We have Morris's work and home phones tapped and there's been no communiqué between them either. Have you seen her at the lab, or heard Morris mention her being away at the moment?'

'Nah, I wouldn't have known he was married 'til you told me. He's all strictly business here, no time for chit-chat. Works long days, sure doesn't seem to spend much time at home. Drives himself to and from the lab and locks himself away in his office at lunch times. I'll see what I can find out about his home life from Brent, the Two-IC here. He's also tons of fun,' Spooky added wryly. 'Neither of these dudes is what you'd call warm-'n-fuzzy. In fact, the only time I see them getting along is when they're huddled over a schematic or a new piece of tech.'

'I'll send you through a photo so you'll know Susan Morris if you see her. If she turns up or you find out anything more, let me know straight away.'

'Will do Ben.'

———

North of Archer River in Cape York, a black Wrangler Renegade Jeep powered along the Peninsular Development Road dragging a long cloud of red bull-dust in its wake. The remote gravel highway stretched as far as the eye could see to the north and south, with lesser roads peeling off it at intervals. At one well-traversed intersection the Jeep slowed and turned, leaving its dusty wake to drift on alone for a short distance and then settle again to await the next vehicle.

After motoring another two kilometres, the red dust-covered Jeep turned into the main street of the small mining town of Lester. With a gritty squeak from its front disk brakes and a rumble of its V8 engine, the Jeep came to a stop in front of the Mount Lester Mining Company's office. The modern, rendered brick office building stood out from the other more modest structures around it, as though serving as a bricks-n-mortar statement about the town's ownership.

Having leased land from Wolverton Cattle Station which covered some fifteen hundred square kilometres of the cape, Mining giant Rio Tinto, owner of MLMC, had constructed the Lester township on the station's northern-most boundary. The tiny town with its green lawns, bitumen roadways, swimming pool, squash court and shopping hub was an oasis in the expanse of sparse savannah landscape.

To the occupants of the Jeep the town came as a welcome relief after hundreds of kilometres of corrugated gravel roads. The Bob Seger song on the stereo stopped mid-chorus as the ignition was switched off and the driver and passenger climbed out of the air-conditioned cabin. They stretched, the lenses of their dark sunglasses fogging up in the outside air. The sun was high in the sky and the humidity was stifling. Almost immediately beads of sweat formed on their skin. As they glanced up and down the main street, noting the absence of other people, they heard a voice behind them call, 'Hello!' Turning, they saw a smartly-dressed woman striding down the footpath toward them, smiling warmly.

'You must be Troy and Josephine?' At their nods she extended a hand. 'I'm PR officer, Veronica Stanley. Welcome to Lester. So, how was your trip?'

'Pretty uneventful,' Wolf drawled, taking her hand in his firm grip. 'Apart from a close encounter with a mob of Brahman cattle.'

'Yeah, you'll see a lot of them out here.' Grinning, Veronica turned to shake Modeen's hand. 'They're inquisitive buggars and not at all shy of traffic.' She ran a critical eye over their dust-covered Jeep and said wryly, 'Nice wheels you got there, but not a great colour to keep clean around these parts.' Jangling a set of keys in her hand, she announced, 'OK, follow me and we'll get you squared away. Someone from HR will collect you in the morning, and take you on an orientation tour of the mine and township.'

Indicating the street with a wave of her arm, Modeen said, 'Where is everyone?'

'The mine operates twenty-four hours a day, seven days a week, on a three shift rotating roster, so at this time of day most of the rock apes are either at work or catching up on sleep before the start of their next shift. Don't worry, you'll get to meet lots of people while you're here.'

Modeen threw her an amused frown. 'Rock apes?'

'You haven't heard miners called that before?'

'No.'

'Well, you'd better get used to it, you're going to hear it a lot and be called that yourself.' She grinned and headed to the white dual cab ute parked beside the office. 'Right, I'll show you to your accommodation. We've stocked it with the makings of tea and coffee and have arranged breakfast, lunch and dinner for you in the wet mess.'

Modeen and Wolf shared a glance as they climbed back into the Jeep. They followed Veronica around the block to a low-set demountable in a fenced yard. The two bedroom structure, clad in light grey colourbond iron, sat a metre off the ground on metal supports. Stairs led to the small front porch and larger back veranda. The residences on either side of it were identical, all relocatable mining homes with a variety of vehicles, boats, wading pools and kids' toys littering their yards.

Wolf pulled into the driveway and turned off the motor as Veronica strode past the Jeep saying brightly, 'Give me a sec, I'll just open up.' As she headed to the front door, Wolf and Modeen sat silently eyeing the place.

After a long moment, Modeen murmured, 'So … our new home. Our first one together.'

Wolf looked over at her, trying to judge her mood, but her expression gave nothing away. Deciding to play it safe, he put a large hand on her knee and said in a low, gravelly voice, 'Yes, but only while it suits us.'

She fixed him with a solemn gaze. 'Let's hope it's far enough away.'

He frowned. 'Not having second thoughts already?'

Turning to stare out the window again she said pensively, 'You saw Ben's report on the fingerprints found on the Lebedev?'

'Yeah, he showed me the folder. I forget the Russian bloke's name, but Ben had a nice mug shot of him, along with photos of two of his known associates. One of them was the Asian with the blue blades.'

'Yes, knife expert Jun Lee Chau. And the other one is long sticks specialist Keith Curbaine. Both masters of Yet-Chuan-Do, a combination of Taekwondo and Chinese martial arts.'

'Well, they might be pretty handy with knives and sticks, but we're not in the *Matrix,* and I haven't come across anyone fast enough to dodge a bullet,' Wolf said confidently.

'Then there's their leader, Vladimir Debeljah, a known member of the Russian Mafia, along with his little brother, Sergio, recently terminated.' She turned to gaze levelly at Wolf. 'And I was the one that terminated him.'

CHAPTER FIVE

Tossing the last of the French fries into his mouth, followed by the remaining few mouthfuls of cola, Bugs crushed the aluminium can in one large, freckled hand and sat back in the driver's seat of his NatSec Aurion. As he flicked the crushed can on top of the pile of rubbish on the passenger's side floor, a grey E400 Mercedes appeared at the top of the main street and the canal phone in his ear crackled.

'Package coming to ya, Bugs.'

'Roger that, Spook. I have the package in sight.' Watching the green Holden ute behind the Mercedes turn off the highway and disappear from view, Bugs wiped his hands on his pants and noted the time.

Twenty-sixteen.

Straightening in his seat, he turned the key in the ignition and pulled the Aurion out of the McDonalds carpark. A sprinkle of rain from out of the darkness activated the vehicle's automatic windscreen wipers as Bugs put a finger to the comms unit in his ear. 'Another fourteen hour shift, Spook?'

'Yeah, they're really busting my hump at the lab.'

'Floggin' the new guy, hey?' Bugs glimpsed a flash of white as the windscreen reflected his trademark toothy grin.

'Seems like it. So, any sign of his missus yet?'

'Nah. Apart from a gardener who rolls up every mornin' and does a coupl'a hours' work, the place is deserted.' Bugs paused to negotiate a turn in the road, careful to stay a reasonable distance behind the Merc. 'It's been a week now, so I'm guessin' if Morris does have a wife, she's probably done a runner. He works long hours 'n wives don't like that. Oh sure, they want the money, but they also want hubby home with them. Y'know when I was married, I was glad to get back on tour after a month at home. It was great for the first coupl'a weeks, but then I'd start feelin' smothered. The ex wanted us to do everythin' together. She wouldn't let me out of her sight for a second, always had to—'

At the sound of loud snoring from the other end of the line Bugs snapped, 'What?'

'C'mon mate.' There was a roll of eyes in Spooky's voice. 'You know, it's not like I haven't heard this one before.'

'Oh man, that's just *cold*.'

Spooky gave a bark of laughter. 'Just telling it like it is.'

'Humph!'

Still chuckling, Spooky said, 'Right-o mate, catch ya in the morning. Call me if you need me.'

With a good-natured, 'Whatever,' Bugs removed his finger from the comms unit.

Ahead of him the Mercedes continued north on the Princess Highway, passing over Shoalhaven River where the highway split into two dual-lane carriageways. As he crossed what was obviously a new traffic bridge, Bugs glanced over at its south-bound counterpart. A cage-like mass of iron and cables, its aged construction was in stark contrast to the modern simplicity of the north-bound bridge. Looking ahead again, he saw the Mercedes turn right at Bolong Road and make a quick left onto Brinawarr Street. He followed, keeping two cars between them, and saw the Merc turn into an expansive driveway in front of a three bay garage.

Driving casually past the residence, he nosed the Aurion onto the side of the road some five hundred metres from the house. After grabbing his backpack and wet weather jacket from off the back seat, he climbed out of the car. With a quick look around to check nobody was taking a moonlit stroll nearby, he strode up to the neatly trimmed hedge running along the property's boundary and pushed his way through the dense foliage. For a big man he moved stealthily, a shadowy figure making his way quickly and silently past the fifteen metre swimming pool, three bay garage, around the back of the conservatory, and into a sheltered garden area close to the main house.

Wondering why he was out in the cold when it appeared he could take up residence in the dark, clearly uninhabited western wing without anyone knowing, he slipped the backpack off his shoulders and rummaged through its contents. Taking out a parabolic listening device, he lowered himself to the ground with his back against the trunk of a tree, tucking the backpack behind himself as a pillow.

After plugging the audio connector of the device into his phone, he tapped on the icon that flashed onto the screen and synchronised the device to the canal phone in his ear. Settling in for the long haul he leaned back with a sigh, running a hand over his strawberry-blonde buzz cut hair.

When a light came on in a room to the right of the conservatory he pointed the reflector in that direction and saw Philip Morris through the window, clearly framed against the kitchen's pale green decor. Pressing the canal phone more firmly into his ear, Bugs gave a silent grunt as the audio streaming to it came through loud and clear. He could hear Morris' footsteps on the tiled floor and the hum of the microwave as he warmed his dinner.

———

The reversing beeper combined with the deep roar of the Caterpillar's huge diesel engine resonated in the bauxite pit as a 776D haul truck backed its mega-belly wagon beneath the bucket of a waiting 992G loader. Once the wagon was in position the loader sounded its horn and began filling the haul truck with the powdery red/brown material.

From the site office overlooking the pit, site supervisor Gus Wright put down his binoculars and turned to the shift foreman who was holding out a steaming mug. Taking it from him with a nod of thanks he muttered, 'The two new recruits are workin' out well.'

'Good,' the foreman replied, cradling his own mug between two stained, work-roughened hands. 'We've got enough dead wood already without adding more.'

'Not often we get a married couple who're both good workers.'

The foreman flicked him a glance. 'They've got different surnames, so I don't think they're married.'

'No? I just assumed....' Gus took a sip of coffee. 'Not that it makes any difference in a remote mining town like this.' The two men shared a knowing glance.

'Yeah, most of the hundred or so single men on site couldn't give a damn either way.' Draining his mug, the foreman set it down on the worn, graffiti-covered lunch table. 'They don't appear an overly affectionate couple. How long do you give 'em?'

Gus gave a snort. 'Wouldn't like to say, but I've seen 'em all out here. Touchy-feely couples joined at the hip, newlyweds already at each other's throats, and married couples who renew their vows only to go their separate ways soon after.' Raising an eyebrow he said drily, 'This is the place to put a relationship to the test, that's for sure.'

'Yeah, it'll either make it or break it.' The foreman grinned.

'Always seems to me people either try too hard or not hard enough to hold onto their relationships,' Gus went on thoughtfully. 'Gotta say, these two appear to have an underlying trust and understanding, they just don't bother to flaunt it.'

The foreman nodded slowly. 'Maybe, but I'm already hearin' some rumbles from the single men's quarters.'

'To be expected I guess, the new bird's a real looker. But the other blokes better back off if they know what's good for 'em. These two are both ex-military.' Gus picked up the binoculars again and watched Wolf dump the last bucket-load of bauxite into Modeen's haul truck. As soon as he backed the loader away, she set off for the loading facility where the bauxite would be transported to Weipa by rail, to be stockpiled there. 'So it wouldn't surprise me,' Gus mused aloud, 'if they do just fine out here.'

As the change of shift siren sounded, most of the trucks, loaders and light vehicles were already on their way to the main concourse behind the office and work-shop facility. As Modeen and Wolf headed for the change rooms the supervisor on the following shift jogged up behind them.

'Wolverton!' When Wolf stopped and turned the supervisor came to stand beside him. 'Harold Evans, afternoon shift supervisor.' He looked flustered and didn't wait for a response. 'You wanna do a doubla?'

'Doubla?' Wolf looked at him blankly.

'Yeah, you know a double shift? We're down a coupl'a miners and need someone who can operate a loader.'

Wolf gazed at him levelly. 'They drummed fatigue management into us during the induction. Doesn't working two consecutive shifts—' He stopped on seeing Evans' expression.

Shaking his head, Evans scoffed, 'Fatigue manage-ment … yet they offer penalty rates that have plenty of blokes breaking their necks to work as many shifts as we'll give 'em! And with most of 'em fly-in-fly-out, there's not much else to do while they're here.' He eyed Wolf assessingly. 'So how about it, you in or out?'

When Wolf raised his eyebrows at Modeen, she shrugged. 'Go ahead if you want to. After all, we're not here on holiday.'

Turning back to Evans Wolf growled, 'OK, I'm in.'

. . .

After Wolf headed back to the site hut, Modeen hurried to catch the shift bus into town. All heads turned her way as she climbed on board and moved down the aisle looking for a spare seat. A few of the men laughingly shoved their friends aside as though to make room for her, but she ignored them, instead taking a seat next to one of the few other females on the bus.

Gail looked to be in her mid-thirties, overweight and with an open, friendly face. She was a haul truck operator, she informed Modeen cheerily. A little rough around the edges judging by the way she held her own with the males in the colourful language and giving cheek departments, but a good person at heart, Modeen decided.

'Y'gotta watch yourself around these horny bastards,' she warned Modeen with a grin.

'If you didn't charge so much, Gail, we wouldn't be so horny!' one of the men shouted.

'Shut-up Sludge, yah randy old coot!' she yelled back. Amid the laughter, she continued. 'Take no notice of 'em, Jo. They talk big but most of 'em are basically harmless.'

The bus pulled up in front of the tavern which seemed to be the town's central hub. While most of the others made for the tavern, talking noisily about having some 'well-earned refreshments', Modeen headed home. Once inside she dropped her work backpack on the floor of the bedroom. After shedding her grubby work gear she changed into snug-fitting leg-ins, a T-shirt and her favourite Nike runners. On second thought, she dug out her Army-issued gaiters and slipped them over her shins before heading out the back door. Once outside she set off on a cross-country run.

The narrow track she'd chosen led her through some dense patches of scrub, and she was thankful for the gaiters' protection against the spinifex under-growth. The track ran for two kilometres and led to a clearing above a steep ridge. Pausing there to catch her breath, she stretched and took in the outback vista before heading back to the recreation centre for a workout in the gym. After a quick dip in the centre's swimming pool, she made her way home to shower and change.

It was eighteen-thirty hours when, dressed in cream cargo pants and a checked shirt, she made her way to the mess hall for dinner. This *en masse* mode of dining, similar to that offered by the military, felt comfortably familiar. There was more variety in the food on offer, however. She was pleased to see fresh eggs as opposed to the powdered variety, and to find the coffee quite drinkable. Most of the men went back for seconds and thirds, which appeared to be the norm.

There were no other women in the mess at that time so she sat on her own, quietly putting away a plate of roast beef and vegetables and a surprisingly light York-shire pudding. Between mouthfuls she glanced at her watch. Wolf wouldn't be home 'til after twenty-three hundred, giving her time to kill. All the same, she didn't want to linger. The hall was filling as the single men poured in, jostling for the spare seats at her table. They were friendly enough, but she wasn't one for small talk at the best of times.

As soon as she'd finished eating she rose to leave. At their murmurs of disappointment she merely called, 'Goodnight,' as she made her way out.

CHAPTER SIX

A month after the initial laser test, Philip Morris was back at the Woomera test facility waiting as the C17 dropped off its precious cargo.

As soon as they were able, he and two technicians climbed into the Oshkosh, which now sported a small glass dome instead of the bulky roof-mounted laser. They headed through the desert to the testing range. Once there, they positioned the vehicle on the same rocky outcrop as before, but this time there was no personnel carrier on the range to target.

With only minimal conversation the three completed the final external checks and then piled back into the cabin, where Morris turned on the targeting computer. The centre console-mounted touch screen blinked into life displaying the US Department of Defence logo. The words *Acquiring target* flashed onto the screen in front of a green radar-like display.

Morris tapped on the comms unit in his left ear. 'Woomera Base, this is FR3. We are good to go.'

'FR3, this is Woomera Base. Airspace has been closed. Taipan One, report.'

At Woomera airfield the rotors of an MRH90 helicopter spun into a blur as it lifted off and then sped low over the desert to buzz the stationary Oshkosh. The vehicle's occupants watched it perform a wide sweep across the test range and then the pilot's voice came over the comms. 'Woomera Base, this is Taipan One. The firing range and airspace are clear. Taipan One, returning to base.'

'Acknowledged Taipan One. FR3, this is Woomera Base. We are OK to go, on your mark.'

Morris tapped the comms unit again. 'Woomera Base, this is FR3. You are clear to arm the targets.'

In the Woomera command tower the range controller lifted a red locking guard and flicked the arming switch to the ON position. Five kilometres to the right of the Oshkosh, an unmanned launch platform rose smoothly to a forty-five degree angle as it prepared to launch the sparrow and sidewinder missiles mounted on it.

Inside the Oshkosh's cabin the words *Targets acquired* flashed up on the touch screen. Hearing dual pings and seeing two dots appear on the radar to the right of their position, Morris announced over the comms, 'Woomera Base, this is FR3. We are GO for launch.'

'Roger FR3. Woomera Base, Fox Two.'

A dark puff of smoke followed by a two metre-long flame erupted from the rear of the sidewinder missile as the propellant of its solid fuel motor ignited, rocketing the missile off the launch platform.

'Woomera Base, Fox One.'

The sparrow AIM-7C missile followed suit, catapulting off the platform and hurtling across the range. Travelling at Mach four, the sparrow soon overtook the slower sidewinder despite being longer and heavier.

Inside the Oshkosh, Morris held his index finger poised over the FIRE button as the two dots raced across the radar screen. Taking a breath and holding it, he tapped the button.

Two red lines representing the laser beam flashed from the centre of the radar to the two dots now parallel with the Oshkosh. The three men recoiled in their seats and shaded their eyes as both missiles erupted in balls of fire and disintegrated, spreading debris across the range in front of them.

Brent and Spooky high-fived each other and Brent gave a long whistle. 'I'd call that a successful test, wouldn't you?'

Spooky looked over at a silent Morris. 'I can't believe how instantaneous that was!'

With a dull-eyed glance his way, Morris said flatly, 'Lasers aren't like projectile weapons, they travel at the speed of light, so you don't have to lead your target.' He looked away again. 'And they aren't affected by wind or gravity. Exact line-of-sight referencing such as this makes hitting a target easier and more effective.'

'More effective? I thought you either hit a target or you don't.'

'Lasers don't have explosive heads like missiles. In this case, the laser beam super-heated the warheads in both missiles and that's what caused them to explode.'

'Well it works a treat.' Spooky's grin faded. 'Though it's a little off-putting not being able to see the laser beam. Without that visual reference how would we know what went wrong if the target didn't explode? We couldn't see if we'd missed by metres or millimetres … or even if the laser fired at all.'

Morris kept his eyes down as he replied in a monotone, 'The targeting system I designed has built-in safety controls and visual references. It displays the laser's path on screen. Once the laser is aligned, there's no need for further calibration.' He lifted his gaze and paused before going on. 'However, it's interesting you should mention that. I received a variation order from the US Department of Defence earlier this week. They're wanting a visual reference for the laser.' He glanced at Spooky and frowned. 'It'd be easy enough to do, I could simply piggy-back a laser diode onto a couple of the redundant fibres I built into the pulse weapon.'

'So … is there a problem with doing that?'

Morris returned his gaze to the front again. 'While it would be useful to see where the beam's going, it's a bad idea having an enemy able to track where it came from.'

'Oh yeah, you'd be giving your position away.'

'Exactly.'

———

The seven-thirty news had just finished when Modeen felt the demountable shake as more than one set of footsteps pounded up the front stairs and onto the porch.

There was a loud rap on the door as a deep voice called, 'Jo, you home?'

Rising, Modeen pulled her Walther PPQ from between the lounge chair cushions and made her way to the door, hugging the walls as she moved. Slipping Walt into the waistband at the back of her tracksuit pants, she opened the door a crack and turned on the porch light. Squinting through the locked security screen door at the four tall, strapping men standing on the porch, she recognised them as her day shift colleagues. Dressed casually, they each held a can of beer. One of them carried the remains of a chilled six-pack that dripped condensation onto the timber deck at his feet.

'It's me, Shane, and some of the guys,' their spokesman said with a grin. 'We thought you might be lonely with Troy working a doubla, so we've come to invite you to the tavern. They're playing the latest Star

Wars film on the big screen tonight. It should be finished just before the afternoon shift bus drops off Troy.' Shane had an open face and a friendly manner, and appeared to Modeen to be genuine.

Opening the door a little wider, she said smoothly, 'Thanks for the thought, but I've got some things I need to catch up on. And Troy might like to see that film too, he enjoys the odd sci-fi. Do they play movies most nights?'

Shane shook his head. 'Nah, only on Fridays. And there's bingo on Mondays and Texas Hold'em on Wednesdays, all well supported as you can probably guess.'

'Yeah.' Modeen smiled and stepped back, preparing to close the door. 'Well, you guys have a good night.'

With a chorus of Thanks and Seeyas, the four men trudged down the stairs and headed for the tavern. One of them glanced back at Modeen's demountable more than once on the way there.

On her own once more, Modeen extracted the PPQ from her waistband and laid it on the coffee table. She stood staring down at it for a long moment. Murmuring the old Special Forces saying about priorities, 'My weapon … my kit … myself,' she decided this would be a good time to strip down the pistol and give it a clean.

· · ·

Once the PPQ was cleaned and freshly oiled, and with nothing worthwhile to watch on TV, she checked the porch light was still on for Wolf and then picked up the novel she'd brought with her. Heading into the bedroom with it, she climbed into bed, tucking the pistol beneath her pillow. It was years since she'd been in the military but she still couldn't settle without having a weapon within easy reach at all times. As the image of a lifeless Sergio Debeljah face-planting into blood-spattered, puke-green carpet sprang to mind, and she recalled the attempt on their lives in Melbourne, she told herself this wasn't the time to break that habit.

Having read a couple of chapters and still wide awake, Modeen put the book down and decided to make herself a hot drink. Not bothering to turn on the lights, she padded barefoot across the floor to the kitchen, only to freeze when her ears picked up a crunch of gravel outside the bathroom window. She stood motionless, listening as the footsteps continued toward the rear of the demountable. Turning, she crept back into the master bedroom and retrieved her PPQ and the long-handled, solid metal torch she'd used during her stint as a security guard.

From there she tiptoed to the spare bedroom, listening for more crunching gravel and following the sounds around to the master bedroom side of the demountable. Creeping to the back door, she carefully opened it and slipped silently down the back stairs, keeping to the grassed lawn as she made her way to the corner of the building. Once there she peeked around the side and saw a dark figure standing at the window of the master bedroom, gripping the sill as he tried to peer through a gap in the curtains. She was pretty sure he was one of the men who'd called in earlier that night with the affable Shane.

She gave an incredulous shake of her head and ducked down the side toward the figure, keeping to the shadows. A moment later she was on him. Sensing her approach he gasped and whirled around, only to be blinded when she shone the powerful torch beam into his eyes. As he flinched and squeezed his eyes shut, she raised the torch and then brought it down, cracking him on the temple with the solid metal hilt. He gave a grunt of pain and collapsed to the ground.

Grabbing a handful of belt at the back of the man's jeans, Modeen dragged him around to the grassed area near the front porch. Under the porch light she rolled him over and checked his pulse. Satisfied he was only out cold she lifted the wallet from his back pocket, checked his ID, and murmured, 'Robert Leighton, Heavy Combination truck driver.'

And resident peeping Tom.

She straightened and tossed the wallet at his feet. She stared down at him and nudged him with a toe. He didn't respond. With a tart, 'Well, Robert Leighton, you can sleep it off right where you are,' she turned and went back inside.

. . .

At twenty-three forty the shift bus stopped at the tavern with a squeal of brakes. Most of its weary passengers had to be woken up to alight, but not Wolf. With a gravelly, 'Thanks mate,' to the driver he climbed out and trudged homeward, looking forward to a shower and bed and wondering if Modeen was still up. As he made his way along the footpath his ears caught the sound of approaching footsteps and he peered into the darkness, to see a man stumbling toward him nursing his head.

When the man drew closer, Wolf drawled, 'That you, Leighton?'

The man flicked him a sideways glance but didn't answer.

Sure he had the right bloke, Wolf said jovially, 'Still out at his hour? Must've been a big night at the pub. Gonna be tough gettin' up in the mornin'.'

Managing a grunt in response, Leighton staggered past, giving Wolf a wide berth. With a bemused shake of his head, Wolf continued on to the demountable.

Feeling the building shudder as heavy footsteps climbed the stairs and hearing a key turn in the lock of the security screen door, Modeen set her book down and sat up in bed. She smiled as Wolf came inside and said warmly, 'Hey Troy.'

'Hey.' As he strode into the bedroom she lifted her

face and he bent to kiss her before dumping his work bag on the floor.

'So, how was your first doubla?'

'Nothin' out of the ordinary, just a longer day.'

'Wanna hot drink?'

'Coffee thanks, after I take a shower.' He peeled off his work shirt, revealing a toned, muscular torso. 'How was your evenin'?'

She couldn't help a lopsided grin. 'Pretty quiet for the most part.'

'The blokes on shift were ribbin' me about keepin' a close eye on you.' Wolf paused to stare narrow-eyed at her. 'Say … I passed one of the blokes on our shift just now, staggerin' home. He was holdin' his head in his hands like he had a massive hangover, but now I'm wonderin'….' He frowned. 'Is there anythin' I need to know?'

Her grin widened. 'No, everything's fine.'

Appearing unconvinced, Wolf growled, 'You'll tell me if I need to take any action?'

She fluttered her eyelashes at him. 'You'll be the first to know. Now go and have your shower while I boil the kettle.'

'We're back in Nowra.' Spooky pressed the mobile closer to his ear as he sat back on the sofa.

'Safe to talk?'

'Yep, I'm in my motel room.'

'Good,' Ben said crisply. 'Report.'

'The test of the new airframe and laser configuration we fitted to the Oshkosh went well. The laser successfully downed two missiles fired across the Woomera range. There are still more mods to be made to it though. Morris was talking about adding a bottom laser turret and then modifying the targeting system to include an integrated helmet-mounted cueing display.'

Ben gave a grunt of acknowledgment. 'At this end I've had the techs analyse the surveillance footage you've sent. It appears Morris is using a spy camera to take photos of the laser's progress and its components, which is consistent with the data the CIA believes is being leaked. We know he uses a pen with a built-in camera to take the photos, but we don't know how he's transmitting the data.'

'Now you mention it … I've noticed he has a habit of fondling the pen in his pocket like he's really attached to it … and no wonder. I'm guessing it'd contain a mini USB connector that would plug into a computer, though I can't say I've seen him do that.'

'The surveillance footage hasn't picked that up either,' Ben cut in. 'And we've been monitoring all his network and phone activity, so he must be off-loading the data by some other means.'

'You know…,' Spooky said pensively, '… I don't see how the data from a few photos could be all that helpful in reconstructing a laser. Even with detailed schematics it'd be a tough ask.'

'Correct. Our analysis of the intercepted data suggests there is insufficient detail for that purpose. That's why we suspect the intention may be to steal the laser once it's completed.'

'Steal the laser? *How?* It's on a military base!'

'Still, we can't afford to be complacent. It's crucial we stay alert for anything that doesn't look, sound, or smell right. Bugs reports there's still no sign of the wife, Susan, so I've instructed him to search the house when the opportunity arises. We're beginning to suspect she's being held hostage in return for her husband's cooperation.'

'Yeah,' Spooky gave a slow nod, 'that's feasible given the situation. So, what's our next move?'

'We have to let it play until we can positively ID who's involved. Ideally, we'd need to locate Susan Morris before we move to intervene.'

'It's gotta be an international cartel if the CIA's involved. Don't they have any idea who's behind it?'

'All they can tell us is that the data was intercepted by one of their Russian operatives, which incidentally coincides with other recent events closer to home.'

'Yeah? What events?'

'Modeen and Wolf bumped heads with a Russian named Vladimir Debeljah in Melbourne, and we believe he and his associates are vying to take over the Black Mamba organisation.'

Spooky gave a snort. 'Patel won't like that!'

'Patel is dead.'

'From the injuries he sustained in the crash?'

'Our intel suggests it was an execution-style killing, and we suspect Debeljah was involved.'

'No loss to the world,' Spooky said drily.

'Agreed, but with Patel out of the picture there's now a power struggle for control of the organisation. It seems the Russians also want the biker gangs to join them … so it appears they're actively recruiting.'

Spooky gave a long whistle. 'We're talking the Russian mafia here, aren't we?'

'It appears so, and the "Bratva" as their mafia is sometimes called, isn't a singular criminal organisation. It's made up of over six thousand individual groups, with more than two hundred of those groups having a global reach. Our intel suggests the Australian contingent is only relatively small at this stage.'

'Wow.' Spooky paused as if to let that sink in before asking, 'So what happens now?'

'You stay on Morris at the lab, Bugs will continue surveillance of Morris's house, and I'll see to it that security is ramped up at Nowra base. We'll have to watch what happens with the Mambas. If the Russians are successful in taking over, it'll indicate that they're better resourced and have greater numbers than we've credited them with to this point. Here's hoping that's not the case.'

As Spooky turned off the highway ahead of him, Bugs slipped into the left lane, four cars back from the grey E400 Mercedes. Sculling another cola, he crushed the empty can and tossed it onto the growing pile on the floor of the passenger's side. With a bored sigh, he stared at the cars ahead, not bothering to close the gap between his Aurion and the Merc. Sure enough, Morris led him along the usual route north on Princess Highway, over the Shoalhaven River, into Bolong Road and then Brinawarr Street.

Motoring past as Morris nosed the Merc into one of

the garage's three bays, Bugs parked down the street again and once more took up position in the leafy garden area between the house and the conservatory. As the subject of his surveillance went about his evening routine, heating up a TV dinner in the microwave, having a shower and going to bed just before midnight, Bugs found himself wishing something would happen to relieve the boredom.

At o-six-thirty, Morris was up again, showered, shaved and on the road. After tailing him to the other side of Shoalhaven bridge where Spooky picked him up and followed him the rest of the way to the lab, Bugs did a U-turn and headed back to Brinawarr Street. After parking the Aurion among other cars on the side of the road so it would look like just another innocuous vehicle, he strolled nonchalantly down the footpath toward Morris' house. Using the thickly wooded area for cover, he made his way to the usual surveillance position in the rear garden. Moving closer to peer through the nearest window on the ground floor, he gave a satisfied grunt. The LED on the room's security monitor was inactive, so the motion sensor was blind to all movement. It appeared Morris had neglected to arm the system before leaving.

Confident he wouldn't be setting off any alarms, Bugs slapped on some surgical gloves and jimmied open the latch on the sash window. A moment later he was inside.

Too easy, Morris. You need to be more security-conscious, buddy.

Moving stealthily through the expansive house, he headed up an ornate timber staircase which led to the upper storey bedrooms. The size of the main bedroom came as a surprise; it was small as far as mansions go. Glancing around, he decided the room was in a section of the original building, which had obviously been renovated and extended. All the same, the bedroom accommodated a king-sized bed, had its own ensuite, two small built-in robes between dormer widows, and one large robe whose sliding mirrored doors encompassed the entire end wall.

With a wry grin Bugs went to the end wardrobe. Murmuring under his breath, 'This'll confirm whether she's still around,' he slid the mirrored doors open, releasing a slightly stale waft of perfume and making the light fabric on some of the clothing inside twitch at the sudden release of air. He stared at the colourful row of dresses and gowns crowding the hanging space, and below them the assortment of high-heels, ankle boots and sandals stacked two high and three deep on the carpeted floor. Raising his eyes to the shelf above the clothes rail, he took in the feathered fascinators, race-day hats, and handbags in various colours stacked there.

He shook his head. 'Guess I was wrong about you, Mrs Morris.'

Glancing at his watch, noting he had about an hour before the gardener arrived, Bugs slid the wardrobe closed. He retraced his steps and once downstairs continued his search. Starting at the conservatory he progressed through the kitchen, meals area, dining, family room, formal dining, formal lounge and into the main foyer at the entrance.

Everything seemed normal. As far as he could tell there was nothing out of place for an upmarket home like this. Pausing briefly to admire the elaborate lead-lighting in the front door and side panels, he turned back down the foyer, only to stop abruptly when his eyes fell on a carved timber hutch.

There, resting on its edge, was a black pen with a gilded centre band and clip. Could this be the pen Ben had briefed him about? Picking it up, he gingerly twisted it apart and saw protruding from the middle of its back section a mini male USB connector. Pulling out his mobile, he plugged the back half of the pen into the phone's mini USB port and saw an icon flash onto the screen. It was labelled FOLDER ONE and dated two days previous. Tapping on the icon, he downloaded the folder onto his phone and emailed it to Ben.

He was slipping the mobile back into a pocket in his black cargoes when a shadow fell across the glass panels of the front door. This was followed by the dark silhouette of a man, and then the sound of a key being inserted into the lock. Moving swiftly and silently, Bugs clicked the pen back together and replaced it on the hutch, before ducking into the formal lounge just as the front door opened.

Sneaking through the formal dining room, Bugs paused at the doorway leading into the entry foyer and pressed himself against the wall. He heard footsteps on the polished timber floor. They stopped in the location of the hutch. After a few moments they headed back to the front door.

Hearing the door open again, Bugs turned on his mobile's camera. He held out the phone so it protruded into the corridor, in time to see the gardener leaving the house.

He's early.

Slipping back into the foyer, Bugs checked the hutch.

The pen had been moved.

With his ears pricked for any sounds of movement, Bugs picked up the pen, twisted it apart, and once more inserted the back section into his phone. FOLDER ONE popped up on the screen again but this time it showed the current date.

He cursed under his breath.

That's how they've been transferring the data.

After quickly downloading the contents of the new folder and emailing them to Ben, Bugs headed for the jimmied window and slipped outside.

I'm done here. Looks like I have another subject to tail.

. . .

Inside the grey Mercedes, Morris selected USB DEVICE from the touch screen in the car's plush centre console and two audio files appeared on screen. When he clicked on the first file a familiar voice issued from the speakers.

A smarmy voice with a Russian accent.

'So far so gudt, Mr Morris. Keep followingk our instructions and you vill see your vife again. Ve vill have further instructions for you soon.'

When the recording ended, Morris tapped on the second audio file.

This time the speaker had an Australian accent … and was female.

'I'm OK, Philip.' Despite her brave words, the woman's voice shook. 'T-they want me to tell you….' She gulped. 'They won't hurt me … as long as you do as they ask.' She rushed on. 'Philip, I lov—' The recording stopped abruptly.

There was nothing else on the file.

Wincing as though in pain, Morris pulled into his usual parking bay at the front of the Advanced Laser Optics laboratory. Disconnecting the back section of his pen from the USB adaptor, he reassembled the pen and slipped it into the inside pocket of his coat. Leaning forward to rest his head on the steering wheel, he whispered wretchedly, 'Susan…'

When Spooky came bounding up to the car with a

concerned, 'You OK, boss?' Morris jerked upright and glowered at him.

Climbing out of the vehicle, he marched stiff-backed toward the lab, barking, 'Have you got the Oshkosh out of storage?'

'Not yet—'

'Well get to it, and park it in the lab.' Gazing forward, Morris said tersely, 'We need to pull the airframe back out and make some more mods.'

Bugs gave a derisive snort as he watched the 'gardener' potter around the Morris premises. Apart from some apathetic clearing of dead leaves off the paths with a leaf-blower, the man didn't accomplish anything much. But then … gardening wasn't what he was there for. Bugs was kicking himself for not noticing that sooner when he felt his mobile vibrate in his pocket. He pulled it out and, after glancing at the caller ID on screen, pressed Answer.

'Hey Ben.'

'Bugs. Can you talk?'

'Yep.'

'The data you sent is exactly the intel we needed. Those files contain irrefutable evidence that Morris's wife is being used as leverage to make him comply with the perpetrators' demands. How did you come by the files?'

'It's the gardener,' Bugs replied flatly. 'Morris puts his pen on the hutch in the front entrance before he leaves in the mornings. Then the gardener rolls up to collect it, and swaps it with a new one.'

'So that's how they're doing it….' Ben paused before saying crisply, 'Right. He's your new best friend. We need to find out where he goes and who he contacts.'

'Already on it,' Bugs replied. 'I've stuck tracker TD5554 on his ute, a white Holden Colorado tray-back. He usually bums around the yard for an hour or so to keep up the charade before headin' off. And don't worry, I'll be on his tail when he leaves.'

'Good work mate, keep me posted.'

'Roger that.'

————

Modeen found settling into the routine of life in the tiny Lester township surprisingly easy. All the same, she continued sleeping with the Walther PPQ under her pillow. Unsure whether such insular small-town life suited her, she conceded it did have its advantages. For one thing, everyone knew everyone else, and any new faces became the talk of the town. And for another, nobody could get up to much without the whole town knowing about it.

Rob Leighton, case in point.

It came as no surprise to anyone, especially

Modeen, to hear Leighton had done a runner. Word was that he'd gotten into a fight on Friday night, copped a hiding, and left town the next morning. The local police also didn't appear surprised when Modeen reported the incident.

After informing her that Leighton was known to them and had a long list of offences, the desk sergeant asked, 'You missing any underwear off your clothesline?' When she shook her head and arched an eyebrow at him, he explained, 'It's just that this creep likes to take souvenirs. Anyway, thanks for reporting him. He hasn't been violent to date, but you never know with these sickos, so we'll put out a bulletin on him all the same.'

On Wednesday, Texas Hold'em night at the tavern, it seemed everyone not on shift had rolled up to try their luck at the tables. As she and Wolf strolled into the hotel, Modeen saw the publican behind the bar grinning and rubbing his hands together, and no wonder. The cashed-up miners were known for being big drinkers, and this could be a long, thirsty night.

Taking seats at different tables so they wouldn't knock each other out of the competition too early, Wolf and Modeen shared a glance. While playing tavern rules wasn't their preferred variant of Texas Hold'em, they joined in for a few reasons. For one, it was simply expected they'd participate. For another, it was an opportunity for social interaction. Besides, playing cards was nostalgic for them, a reminder of their time in the military when playing poker was a welcome distraction during the regular 'hurry up and wait' periods between sorties.

The tables filled quickly, and at nineteen hundred hours dealing began. The knock-out competition rules that saw the blinds exponentially raised after every round, ensured play didn't continue all night. So by twenty-two hundred the ten tables had reduced to just one table of nine.

Modeen was one of those nine.

Ignoring the taunts from ousted beer and rum-guzzling miners about beginner's luck being the only reason a *woman* could make it through to the final table, she sat quietly winning enough hands to stay in the competition.

Wolf stood to one side watching her with a knowing grin twitching the corners of his mouth. He was well aware of Modeen's skill with cards, having lost to her a number of times himself. He'd also seen her teach more than one cocky new Army recruit how to play. All the same, in light of the increasingly exorbitant blinds forcing contestants to play hands they normally wouldn't, he conceded that luck did play a large part in deciding the overall winner.

And it wasn't Modeen.

However, before being knocked out she gave them all a good run for their money. And as she rose to leave the table after a final losing hand, she dipped her head at the remaining contestants in a mark of respect. Joining Wolf at the bar, she grinned up at him and received a quick, beefy-armed hug and a gruff, 'Well played.'

The next big event in town was Thursday night Bingo at the tavern, followed by Saturday afternoon barefoot lawn bowls at the local club, both well patronised. The townsfolk were aware of the importance of making their own fun in a remote town. For miners not on a fly-in-fly-out basis there were also trips to the cape for fishing charters and croc-viewing, while other die-hards went feral pig-hunting.

On their first rostered days off, Modeen and Wolf packed the Jeep and drove the two-and-a-half hours to Weipa. They stayed there overnight, dining at the popular bowls club, and then spent a carefree morning browsing the shops, sipping half-decent espresso coffees, and taking in the beach and the bauxite-red surrounding landscape. While nobody would describe Weipa as a big city, the break from the confines of Lester proved to be therapy for what Modeen called 'cabin fever.'

———

At NatSec headquarters in Melbourne, Ben leaned back in his chair with his eyes glued to the tracking app on his mobile phone. He watched a green dot with the tag

TD5554 and blue dot TD9308 heading north out of Nowra on the Princess Motorway. Zooming out to get a wider view, he gave a thoughtful frown.

If they stay on the motorway they might be heading to Wollongong. Or maybe….

His eyes narrowed and he minimised the tracking app before dialling his NatSec counterpart in the Sydney office.

Bugs sighed and rubbed his eyes. Three cars ahead of his Aurion, the white Colorado tray-back had passed through Wollongong and was now approaching the southern outskirts of Sydney. The crackle of the comms unit in his ear made him sit up as an unfamiliar voice said, 'Barry, it's Craig, Charlie Team. You receiving, over?'

Bugs grinned. Craig Houston was one of NatSec's more amiable, though still highly skilled, agents.

'Craig, long time, buddy. What's up?'

'I've been sent to relieve you. Your team leader tells me you need to sleep occasionally.' Bugs gave an amused grunt as Craig continued. 'I'm on your six and have the Colorado in sight.'

Checking his rear-view mirror, Bugs glimpsed another black Aurion a few cars back. As though aware it had his attention the sedan accelerated, changed lanes and slipped alongside him. The driver, a thirty-something man with short, dark hair and an equally dark, neatly trimmed beard, threw him a smile and a lazy salute.

Bugs returned the salute. 'Good to seeya, mate,' he announced into the comms. 'Gotta say a bit of shut-eye sounds appealin'.'

'Right, I'll take it from here. Go and get some sleep, buddy.'

'It's all yours.' Lifting his foot off the accelerator, Bugs let the car slip back and watched Houston's Aurion take his place in the lane. When his phone buzzed in his pocket, he hit the Answer icon on his vehicle's stereo touch screen and Ben's voice came through the speakers via Bluetooth.

'Bugs, I've organised Craig from Charlie Team to take over from you.'

'So I see.'

Hearing the weariness in Bugs' voice Ben said, 'Stop in Sydney and get some rest. I'll contact you at eighteen hundred with further instructions. And make sure you catch some sleep, I may need you to do more surveillance work tonight.'

'Roger that.' As he spoke, Bugs was already changing lanes, preparing to take the next off-ramp.

His eyes were stinging as he made for Sydney's central business district. After crossing Tom Ugly's Bridge he decided enough was enough and pulled into the first motor inn he came across. Eighteen kilometres from the CBD, Blakehurst wasn't what most would call one of Sydney's upmarket suburbs, and the motor inn was a long way short of the Ritz. As he opened the door to his assigned unit a rank smell greeted Bugs, along with some scurrying sounds and movement in the darkish corners of the room. Too tired to care, he decided the stench was just sour milk, and told himself he'd dealt with worse things in the past than a few roaches. And at least he was on the right side of George's River.

Not bothering to shower or change he took a quick check of his phone, dropped onto the bed, and was almost instantly asleep.

When the Colorado turned left onto Heathcote Road and exited the highway, the black Aurion followed a few cars behind. Craig took care to stay well back from his quarry as they motored onto the New Illawarra Road. After passing through Punchbowl, Chullora, and Lidcombe, they turned left onto the Great Western Highway heading toward Parramatta.

Once there, the Colorado turned into Pitt Street and then Pitt Lane, which offered rear access to a number of small, high-density apartment blocks. Halfway down the lane the Colorado slowed and then took a narrow, cobblestone ramp that disappeared beneath a three storey block of units.

Idling the Aurion past the unit block, Craig could see the lane was too narrow for street parking, and most of the buildings only had bays to accommodate two or three vehicles at most. He drove to the end of the lane where it met Steele Street and stopped at the intersection, staring at the cemetery across the road while considering his next course of action.

Coming to a decision, he turned right and accelerated to the intersection of Steele Street and the Great Western Highway. When he spotted a break in the traffic he charged across the four lane carriageway with a squeal of tyres, and then ducked into Parramatta Park, nosing the Aurion to a spot under a tree where he could see the front of the unit block.

Taking out his mobile, he checked the tracking app which enabled him to keep track of the Colorado even when he'd lost visual of it. Glad to find it hadn't moved from the apartment block, he reached into the glove box and pulled out a pair of Steiner Tactical binoculars. Putting them to his eyes, he surveyed the front of the building.

Made of sand-coloured brick, it looked to be around twenty years old, and slightly more modern than the neighbouring complexes. The two front units on each level had small verandas that shared common walls and were flanked by what appeared to be master bedrooms, with tiny Juliet balconies. Judging by the letterboxes mounted in the brick front fence, a number of which were overflowing with junk mail, Craig estimated the complex contained twelve apartments in total.

The front units all had their blinds and curtains

closed. He checked the perimeter. There was no sign of movement. He was about to reach for his parabolic listening device but then paused, aware the road noise from the busy highway between him and the building would render the audio virtually useless.

He'd need to take up a better position.

When his phone vibrated with an incoming call, he checked the caller ID before answering, 'Houston.'

'What's your status, Craig?' Ben barked.

'I've followed the Colorado to a unit block in Parramatta. As yet I haven't been able to ascertain which apartment the subject went into, or if he met with anyone. The street address is—'

'Pitt Lane,' Ben cut in, adding by way of explanation, 'I've been tracking you, and the Colorado. So, what's the building's security like?'

'Appears to be pretty tight. Main access is via a basement carpark off Pitt Lane, which is quite narrow. There's a solid metal roller door on the carpark entrance and a security camera mounted above it.' Craig put the binoculars to his eyes again and re-examined the building. 'There are two gates in the solid brick fence at the front of the property, facing the highway. These open into the courtyards of the ground level units. There are two cameras mounted high up under the eaves, which I guess cover the whole front area.' He lowered the binoculars and frowned. 'It's gonna be hard getting close without being seen.'

'Stay out of sight for now, Craig.' Ben sounded

thoughtful. 'All we've been able to determine so far is that the unit block is owned by the Matryoshka Group, a real-estate conglomerate based in Auckland, New Zealand. I'm organising some satellite time which should give us an idea of how many people are in the building.'

'Right-o. I'll head around to the lane again, Ben. I have a better view from there and should be able to see if anyone else rolls up at the complex.'

'Good, but remain out of sight. It's imperative we don't tip them off at this stage. We still have no idea where they're holding the hostage.'

As Ben signed off, Craig nosed the car onto the highway and headed for the traffic lights at the Pitt Street intersection. This time, instead of driving up Pitt Lane, he went around the block and into Steele Street, where he parked alongside the cemetery.

Climbing out of the car, dressed in a smart black business suit and looking every bit the professional, he moved casually around to the boot and retrieved a small overnight bag. Throwing it onto the back seat of the Aurion he followed it inside, to emerge a short time later looking very different in dark glasses and a plain blue polo shirt over baggy jeans.

CHAPTER NINE

Business was slow at Weipa Bowls Club with just the odd tourist in attendance, along with the usual complement of bar flies sitting hunched over their schooners and sharing desultory conversation with anyone and no one. This was the norm for a weekday afternoon in the town's favourite watering hole. On Fridays the club came alive as the town's population swelled with people collecting – and spending – their welfare payments, and workers celebrating the end of the working week. Big by Weipa standards, the clubhouse was well maintained and clean. And the air-conditioning ran twenty-four hours a day.

Rob Leighton sat by himself in the artificial coolness, staring moodily into a quarter-full schooner of beer and ignoring all attempts by the other bar flies to engage him in slurred conversation. He'd said enough already.

Too much, perhaps.

It was all the beer's fault, for loosening his lips.

The bartender threw him a cursory glance. Though Leighton was well known in town, having knocked about the cape region for years, he was notorious for initiating many a drunken altercation, and wasn't well liked. Now, having suffered through a long, self-pitying story about the origins of his badly bruised and swollen face, and then a barrage of abuse for failing to re-fill his glass the instant he drained it, the barman left the tipsy Leighton to drink alone.

When two bikers in dusty black leathers and boots sauntered up to the bar, the one closest to the morose Leighton nudged him on a shoulder with a closed fist. 'Hey, Leighton. You on a day off?'

Turning, Leighton squinted woozily at the grey-bearded, lined and road-grimed face staring into his own.

'What the hell happened to you?' The biker pointed a grubby finger at him and gave a bark of laughter, revealing stained, gappy teeth. He elbowed his companion. 'Check 'im out, will ya? Appears our mate 'ere copped a whack to the head.'

Looking over, the second biker gave an amused grunt. 'It's improved his looks.'

'Yeah.' His grey-bearded mate grinned. 'Then again, the buggar couldn't get any uglier.'

A dark flush crept into Leighton's broad, acne-scarred face. He quickly turned away, not bothering to respond.

The watching bartender, seeing an opportunity to get back at the boorish mongrel, announced loudly and with more than a little relish, 'Apparently, there's a new honey in Lester, a tall blonde who's a real looker. And we all know how much our mate Rob here loves blondes … and brunettes … and redheads.' With a smug grin at Leighton he added, 'Rob was only trying to be *friendly*, but her muscle-bound boyfriend hit him from behind with an iron bar.' He threw the smirking bikers a wink. 'It was a totally *unprovoked* attack.'

Grey beard gave another belly laugh and roared, 'BULLSHIT! More than likely ol'mate here was up to his usual tricks.' He thumped a scowling Leighton on the shoulder and leaned in so their heads were level. 'Pervin' again were ya, son? Y'know, the ladies don't like that … at least not the ones what *are* ladies.' Thumping him again, the biker straightened, sniggering, 'And you're such a wuss, I'm bettin' it was *her* what beat the crap outta ya.'

Amid the eruption of laughter that followed, a crimson-faced Leighton sculled his beer, threw some money on the bar, and scurried for the exit swearing under his breath.

Still chuckling, the bartender turned to the bikers. 'Now, what can I get ya?'

'We'll 'ave two Schooners of mid-strength,' grey

beard said with an amused snort, 'and the rest of that story.'

'Right-o.' After pouring two fifteen ounce glasses of ice-cold, amber beer and placing them in front of his two new patrons, the barman leaned both arms on the bar. 'Leighton talks big, so I take his stories with a whole *bag* o' salt. But I reckon there must be some truth in this one, at least about the woman. The last few weeks I've been hearin' about some new truck-drivin' blonde over at Lester.' He frowned thoughtfully. 'Doesn't take much to excite a camp full of single men, any new female will get 'em goin', but apparently this bird's turnin' everyone's heads.'

Grey beard swallowed a mouthful of beer, burped, and wiped the back of a hand over his mouth. 'Oh yeah?'

The bartender nodded. 'Sure we got some lookers here in Weipa, but when this honey turned up in Lester with her "muscle-bound boyfriend" as Leighton called 'im, she really got the tongues waggin'. Apparently they were both in the military and got the medals to prove it, so she must be reasonably tough.'

A glance passed between the two bikers and then grey beard growled, 'The military, you say?'

'Yeah. Guess it's fair enough for him to join the rock-apes out here, but strikes me as a little unusual she'd be into it too. In my experience, most nice-lookin' babes – the princess types who don't want to get their hands dirty or risk breakin' a nail – opt for office work.

But not this bird, apparently.' Seeing a new customer approaching, the barman straightened. 'Anyway, it'll be interesting to see how long these newbies stick it out. If the heat doesn't get to 'em, the remoteness probably will. They're city-slickers, just moved up here from Melbourne.'

The bikers shared another glance and downed their drinks.

———

At a knock on the door, Vladimir Debeljah yelled, *'Priyekhat!'* and leaned forward to finger the touch pad of his laptop.

An Asian man hurried into the room and announced without preamble, 'We've just received word about the two we targeted in Melbourne. They've been located in Cape York, Queensland, in a town called Lester. It's about....' The man paused as though considering whether or not to continue. 'It's about two hours … from Weipa.'

Debeljah threw himself back in his chair and bared his teeth at the man. 'WHAT?' Thumping the desk with a meaty fist he barked in a thick Russian accent, 'Zis cannot be right, Jun! How ze *hell* did zey find out?'

The Asian waved an open hand in a calming gesture and said soothingly, 'I don't think they know. From what our source tells us, they're living there and working at the bauxite mine. It appears they may not be working for national security anymore.'

Muttering, 'Is too much of coincidence,' Debeljah shook his head.

When he said nothing more the Asian enquired carefully, 'What do you want done?'

'Eezer vay, I vant zem dead.'

'I'll send Uri and Mikhail.' The Asian bowed his head and made to leave but stopped in his tracks when Debeljah growled, *'Ne-et!* I vant zem to stay viz ze prisoner. You go and take Curbaine viz you. I vant zeir heads, Jun, no mistakes zis time.'

'Yes, Vladimir.'

'Ven it is done, I vant all of you to move ze prisoner back to Cairns. Make sure you keep her secure, ve need her… for a leettle longer.'

———

Feeling a light touch on the back of his freckled hand, Bugs opened one eye to see a large cockroach scurry over his watch, up his arm, and then across the bed sheet. Opening his other eye, he checked the time.

Eighteen hundred hours, better check-in with Ben. That roach was right on time with its wake-up call.

Sitting up, he grabbed the mobile from the bedside table. On glimpsing another of the scaly brown pests scuttling over the foot of the bed, he muttered under his breath, 'Oh yeah, this place is a real gem.'

Clicking on the tracking app, he checked the location of TD5554. The Colorado was stationary, still parked in Pitt Lane as when he last checked. He dialled Ben's number and while waiting for him to answer, watched another roach crawl over the grubby carpet and disappear beneath the TV stand.

Ben answered after the second ring and got straight down to business. 'Bugs, I need you to tag-team with Craig. He's in Steele Street, Parramatta, at the end of Pitt Lane.'

'Roger.'

'Watch the premises closely,' Ben went on, 'and keep track of who comes and goes. You should see the gardener exit at some stage heading back to Nowra with new instructions for Morris. Do not approach him, maintain surveillance on the premises. The satellite thermal imaging has identified seven heat signatures in the building, all male. This suggests Susan Morris is not being held there, but this location is our best lead so far.'

'Got it.'

'That's it for now. Craig will fill you in on any further developments at changeover. And he'll be back in the morning to relieve you again.'

'Right, Ben. Will be on my way shortly.'

'Stay out of sight, Bugs, we can't afford to tip them off.'

'Roger that.' Bugs put down the phone, got out of bed and made his way into the bathroom. Standing at the pedestal, he glanced around the room. Fresh towels hung on the rail but a sour smell emanated from the shower recess. Some of the floor tiles were missing, and the folds in the mouldy plastic shower curtain were stuck together with soap scum. The once white grout was stained dark with mould from the base of the recess to half way up the wall, and above the shower rose damp moisture stains radiated from a rough-edged hole in the ceiling.

Staring up at it, Bugs shook his head and muttered, 'Gotta be how the roaches are gettin' in.' He flushed the toilet and washed his hands in the chipped vanity basin. At least the water was nice and hot, so he decided a shave and freshen up would be preferable to taking a shower in the mould pit.

Heading out later with his overnight bag by his side, he was surprised to find someone manning the check-in counter.

Note to self — never pay for a room in advance.

About to make his way out, he paused when the woman standing at the counter raised her voice. It was obvious she wasn't happy about something, and Bugs was pretty sure he knew what.

The man behind the counter was staring down his nose at the woman. Bald and unshaven, he looked to be in his early sixties. An impressive beer gut spilled over his baggy track pants, and tufts of silver fur protruded from the top and sides of his scruffy, off-white singlet.

Bugs eyed the man, thinking that while he didn't look like a manager, he projected disdain like the best of them, and his scruffy appearance fit well with the establishment's overall ambience.

'I keep tellin' you, lady,' the man was saying, 'we don't 'ave cockroaches 'ere. We spray for the buggars every year. An' maybe this ain't the Ritz, but we don't charge like 'em neither.'

The two of them turned as Bugs lobbed his room key onto the counter. The woman was frowning, her face flushed and her lips compressed in a tight line. Giving her a nod, Bugs leaned one elbow on the desk and reached his free hand behind the back of his neck. The manager frowned quizzically at him as Bugs brought his hand forward, slamming it onto the worn, laminate countertop between them.

Bugs raised one eyebrow and fixed him with a narrow-eyed, disapproving gaze. The man had opened his mouth as if to speak but then backed away, watching as Bugs pointedly lifted his hand and then strode off. With a sigh of relief the manager turned his attention to the woman once more.

She was standing, arms crossed, staring at him with a triumphant gleam in her eyes. 'No cockroaches, hey?' she said smugly, pointing to the countertop. 'So how do you explain *that?*'

Glancing down at the freshly splattered cockroach

smeared across the laminate, the manager's shoulders drooped. After blowing a long, drawn-out breath he muttered sourly, 'So … twenty bucks off sound fair?'

Bugs pulled out of the burger joint's drive-through with two bacon-and-egg muffins and two regular coffees. Although it was getting dark, he'd just woken up, so this meal felt like breakfast. He frowned down at the ever-growing pile of rubbish on the car's floor, but then a rueful smile tugged the corners of his mouth.

Sure it's untidy, but at least there's no roaches. Not that they're the worst critters I've had to contend with on different tours of duty.

Driving sedately along Steele Street, he nosed his Aurion next to Craig's. There was no sign of the other agent so he shot off a quick text: *I'm at the car.*

Moments later a dark figure crossed the road at the end of Pitt Lane and jumped into the passenger's seat next to Bugs, spreading his legs around the pile of rubbish on the floor and exclaiming, 'What the—?'

'Yeah … sorry about that.' Bugs flashed him a toothy grin. 'Here, I brang ya a coffee.'

Frowning, Craig took the cardboard cup from him. 'I take it you've been on this stakeout for a while?'

'You could say that.'

'By the size of this pile,' Craig said drily, 'I'd say about a month.'

Bugs gave a throaty chuckle. 'Oh man, you're

good.' Pulling out his mobile, he checked the tracking app and his expression grew serious. 'So ol'mate with the Colorado hasn't gone anywhere?'

'Nah. There was a delivery just now of what looked to be about ten pizzas, which is consistent with the number of blokes Ben said are in the building. Apart from that, nobody has come or gone. There are cameras covering the whole front yard and one at the back just above the double roller door, so be careful. Ben doesn't want them tipped off about our presence. I've been keeping watch from down the side of the complex next door.'

Craig took a sip of coffee and gave an approving grunt before continuing. 'They tend to gather in the top floor apartment at the front of the building. I've been able to record some audio but they're mostly speaking Russian so I have no idea what's being said. I've been emailing the files to Ben in case there's something worthwhile in them. You got a listening device with ya?'

Bugs nodded, his mouth full of the second bacon-and-egg muffin.

'Good, record as much as you can, you never know what might be useful. As usual, if there are any comings or goings, or anything out of the ordinary, Ben wants you to report it.' As he opened the car door, Craig raised his cup to Bugs in a salute. 'Thanks for the coffee, mate. Seeya in the morning.'

CHAPTER TEN

The street lights blinked on as the sun slipped below the horizon and dusk settled over Nowra. Inside the Advanced Laser Optics lab, the intense fluorescent lighting rendered the outside world a dark, formless void for the busy lab workers.

Placing the seventeen millimetre socket of the torque wrench onto the last bolt of the lower turret coupling securing it to the pulse laser assembly, Spooky leaned on the handle of the wrench, releasing the pressure when he heard and felt it click at one hundred and ten newton metres.

Beside him, Brent held out one end of a power conduit. 'Right, now hook 'er up. We'll run a diagnostic to ensure she's in sync with the upper turret and targeting system. If all goes well, we'll be able to mount 'er back on the Oshkosh tomorrow.'

Nearby, at the lab's main workbench, Morris sat

hunched over his laptop. A USB-C adaptor connected the computer to the black 'Scorpion' helmet on the bench beside it. When a three dimensional picture of the fighter pilot's helmet appeared on the laptop's screen, showing a high-tech heads-up targeting display, Morris lifted the helmet and panned it around. On the bottom half of the computer screen an image of the lab, transmitted there from the helmet's high definition camera, followed the movements. With a satisfied sniff, Morris donned the helmet. It was a snug fit, he had to force it down over his head.

Spooky watched, thinking that for a weedy little man Morris had a big noggin.

Once the helmet was in place, Morris pressed control-shift-enter on his laptop and a green heads-up display super-imposed over the camera feed at the bottom of the monitor. He pressed ESC and the display filled the entire screen. Lowering two optical adaptors – being a Trekky, he thought of them as Borg-like – from the brim of the helmet, he clamped them into position over his eyes.

The amplified illumination had his pupils immediately constricting, and he screwed his eyes shut against the glare while hastily flipping down the dark-tinted visor. When he opened his eyes again, he saw the vivid green heads-up display projected onto the interior of the optical adaptors.

He turned his head, panning the camera around the lab. Cross hairs followed the helmet's every movement and a digital display showed distance to target and other targeting information. When he focussed his gaze on the clock mounted above the door on the far wall, the display returned a distance to target of fourteen point eight three metres.

Turning back to the bench, Morris tapped the touchpad on the laptop. Then, keeping his head still, he moved his eyes left to right, up and down. In addition to following the movements, the cross hairs also mirrored the close-in and distant focusing of his eyes. With a satisfied nod to himself, Morris removed the helmet.

Blinking, he placed it back onto the bench and glanced over at Brent and Spooky. 'How're you going with the turret?'

Brent stood next to the airframe, eyes fixed on his laptop's screen. 'She's bolted in place,' he called. 'I've just flashed the new targeting firmware to the ECU and am about to run the diagnostic.'

Morris nodded. 'Good. We'll call it a night when that's done, and start afresh in the morning.'

Keeping his head down and his steps light, Bugs made his way along the fence to take up position as Craig had done, down the side of the neighbouring building. He found a fork in the boughs of a thickly branched, leafy tree that offered an adequate view of the driveway into the Parramatta unit complex and a good vantage point for audio capture. The spot was also broad enough to accommodate him and the parabolic reflector of his listening device.

At twenty-two thirty a Hyundai i30 came to a stop in Pitt Lane and nosed its way down the sloping driveway. With his mobile phone's camera in night vision mode, Bugs zoomed in on the car's two Caucasian occupants, both male. After texting the photo to Ben, he steadied himself against the wide bough behind him and, using the audio device, tracked the new arrivals' movements through the building.

As the last light in the block of units was doused, Bugs repositioned his back more comfortably against the bough and glanced at his watch. It was after midnight, and the only noises being captured by the audio device were snores and the sounds of other night-time bodily functions. At one particularly loud, unpleasant sound, he grimaced, thankful he wasn't inside the building, and then his lips split in a toothy grin as he wondered what Ben would make of that piece of audio.

At o-five thirty, the strident chime of an incoming text message jerked Ben awake. He reached for the mobile with one muscular arm, the other one being trapped under his sleeping wife's head. She was curled against him, her hair a tousled, sweet-smelling fan across his bare chest. He fumbled with the phone one-handed, not wanting to disturb Emily who'd got up to Chelsea during the night. Thankful when she murmured in her sleep and rolled over, releasing his other arm, he blinked and focused on the message.

It was from Bugs: *Gardener just left.*

Ben's lips tightened.

So, the go-between is making his way back to Nowra.

Opening the tracking app on his phone, Ben watched the blip that was the white Colorado turn onto Pitt Street heading south. Switching back to the texting app, he sent a reply: *Acknowledged.*

At just before o-seven hundred Bugs yawned, dragged a hand through his dew-moistened hair and stretched as best he could in his damp, cramped perch. The audio device was faithfully relaying the sounds of early morning activity from the block of units; the whistle of a boiling kettle and the clatter of breakfast crockery. At the thought of breakfast, Bugs' stomach gave a low growl, so he was pleased when a text arrived from Craig minutes later: *Meet me at the car.*

Bundling all his gear back into the canvas and leather roll-out bag, he slipped down from the tree, landing stiffly. Stifling a groan, he had a proper stretch and wondered if his back was now the same shape as the bough. Then, moving quietly and staying in the shadows, he made his way to Craig's Aurion which was once more parked alongside his at the cemetery.

With his slicked-back hair still damp from a morning shower, and wearing clean, neatly pressed clothes, Craig grinned at him from the driver's seat and held up a takeaway coffee.

Bugs gave him a thumbs-up and hurried around to the passenger's side. Jumping in, he took the offered cup and licked his lips, murmuring, 'Thanks man, you're a lifesaver.'

'No probs.' Craig eyed him critically. 'You look like crap, by the way. And you smell like…,' and he leaned in to sniff, '… a wet dog.'

Bugs gave a droll, 'Humph,' and proceeded to drain his cup while Craig looked on with mild, empathetic amusement. 'Oh yeah…,' Bugs crooned, '… that was good.' He crushed the now empty cup and was about to toss it onto the floor when he saw a frowning Craig extend a hand.

'Give it here.'

Handing it over with a sheepish grin, Bugs said, 'Right, to business.' Unfolding his small canvas kit, he rolled it out between them and removed the mobile phone. 'These two arrived late last night in a white Hyundai i30.' He held up the phone for Craig to see.

After studying the image, Craig said pensively, 'Can't say I recognise them.' He glanced at Bugs. 'Did you send it to Ben?'

'Yep, and some audio as well. Heard 'em workin'

out on the ground floor after you left. Must be a gym down there.'

Nodding his understanding, Craig examined Bugs' kit. 'Where're your goggles?'

'In the boot.'

'You should keep 'em with you. I always do.'

'Nah, night vision goggles are part of my tactical gear and I like to keep that all together.'

Craig gave a dismissive headshake. 'Not night vision goggles, *phone* goggles.'

When Bugs looked at him blankly, Craig handed him back his bag and reached behind to grab his own kit from the back seat. Unfolding it on his lap, he took out a pair of slimline goggles and slipped his mobile sideways into the cradle across the front of them.

'With these you can Bluetooth the audio from the dish to your phone, your comms, or plug it in here,' and he pointed to an audio jacket on the goggles. He continued, indicating the other features as he went. 'This button's for taking pictures, and this one's to start and stop the audio. You can also cycle through thermal and night-vision mode here.'

An awed Bugs murmured, 'That's cool. I'll have to ask Ben to get me one.'

'Don't worry, I'll bring you a pair tomorrow.' Craig removed his mobile from the goggles. 'You'll need to upload the latest firmware to your phone, so I'll send you the files.'

Moments later Bugs' phone vibrated with the

incoming text. Busy downloading the attachments he muttered, 'Thanks, mate.'

'No probs.' Craig bundled up his kit. 'Now I'd better get on the job.' Opening the car door, he threw Bugs a teasing grin. 'Do us all a favour, mate, have a shower and get some shut-eye. I'll catch'ya tonight.'

With another mock-insulted, 'Humph,' Bugs got out of the vehicle and strode to his own Aurion, while Craig made his way down Pitt Lane and merged into the shadows. Unlocking the car, Bugs climbed into the driver's seat where he sat for a few minutes, using his mobile to check for a hotel close by.

He was tired enough for any place to do, except maybe the 'La Cucaracha' of the night before. The four star Mantra Parramatta, located just down the highway from his location, came up among the options. Imagining he could already smell the aromas of bacon and eggs, warm buttered toast and freshly brewed coffee, he pictured the king-sized bed – sans eight-legged wildlife – and fluffy white towels in a sparkling clean bathroom.

Yep, the Mantra would do nicely.

———

'Don't be long, Luke,' Philip Morris called, sounding stressed and annoyed. 'We're heading back to Woomera tonight and need to install a new gen-set before we go.'

At the doorway, Spooky turned and called back, 'No worries, boss, I'll be half an hour max,' and ducked out. He'd been going 'out for lunch' for the last few days, but it seemed to irritate Morris even more today.

He went all the same.

With Bugs away in Sydney someone else had to download the files conveyed to and from Morris' place by pen. Ten minutes there, five minutes to download and text off the files, ten minutes to get back, with a quick sandwich eaten en route.

Thirty minutes, tops.

When Ben downloaded the latest audio files from Nowra, one file with instructions for Philip Morris, another with a message from Susan Morris, he breathed a sigh of relief.

She was still alive yesterday … assuming the date stamp on the audio file is correct.

He replayed the message containing the instructions to Morris. While vague, it suggested something was going to happen … that night.

Did we miss an earlier message?

He frowned and shook his head.

Too late now for second guessing.

He sent Spooky a text: *Proceed as planned. Eyes on Morris at all times.*

Opening the tracking app on his phone, he saw the Colorado turning into Pitt Street. There'd be a text from

Craig shortly advising of its arrival at the unit complex. Dropping his mobile onto the desk, he picked up the landline and dialled Woomera Military Base.

'Smith, NatSec,' he said gruffly. 'Put me through to head of security.'

———

Spooky arrived back at the lab to find Brent at the controls of the overhead gantry crane. He was offloading a big red metal box, the gen-set, from a flat bed Hino truck. The diesel-powered electric generator had a control panel at the front, exhaust stack on top, and power sockets for the laser unit fitted at its sides. Walking beside it, Brent carefully lowered the gen-set into position behind the Oshkosh.

Squatting to examine the base of the gen-set, Spooky saw it was already fitted with attachments for the rail system on the Oshkosh's tray. It wouldn't be difficult to install at all. He rose when Morris walked up to examine the generator and enquired, 'Why are we swapping out the gen-set now, when we're heading to Woomera tonight?'

With an impatient headshake, Morris snapped, 'It's not our place to ask questions, just to do as we're told. I thought I'd made that clear.' He eyed Spooky sharply and then pointed to the back of the Oshkosh. 'Now get up there and unhitch the old unit.'

With a shrug, Spooky climbed nimbly onto the back

of the Oshkosh, which was basically a heavy-duty, all-terrain flat bed truck. The laser was one piece of a two-part modular unit fixed to a rail system behind the cab, with the gen-set the second piece. When it was clamped in place behind the laser, the equipment filled most of the tray's full length.

Locking clamps on each side ensured the apparatus didn't slide back and forth on the rails and also made it easy to remove. Hooking up the crane via the lifting points was easy too, but the minor mods made to the laser unit, like the addition of the bottom turret, meant it needed to be installed sideways for testing purposes.

Spooky sighed. The Globemaster was due to arrive at twenty-one thirty. By the time they got the huge transport plane refuelled and the Oshkosh loaded on board, it would be midnight before they took off for Woomera.

CHAPTER ELEVEN

Ben's phone vibrated with an incoming call.

'Four vehicles leaving the unit in convoy, including the white Colorado,' Craig announced without preamble. 'Nine individuals, all Caucasian males. That must've about emptied the building. Do you want me to tail them?'

'Yes,' Ben said curtly, 'but stay back. And let me know if any of them leave the convoy. I'll wake Bugs, get him to search the unit and then catch up with you.'

'Roger.'

Breathing in deeply, Bugs rolled over and stretched his limbs as far as they would go. Even at full stretch, they didn't extend to the edges of the king-sized bed. He put both arms behind his head and lay staring at the unblemished white ceiling. Compared to the dump in

Blakehurst, the Mantra was more like a five star hotel than a four. After a much-needed shower in the pristine bathroom and a few hours of deep REM sleep, he felt like a new man.

And just as well, for Ben rang only a few relaxed minutes later.

Back at the recently vacated Parramatta unit block, Bugs parked in the same spot next to the cemetery and made for the usual tree. This time, instead of positioning himself in the fork, he used the tree's elevation to leap the fence. Sprinting to the building, he flattened himself against the brick wall and stopped to listen in case an alarm was raised.

Everything stayed quiet.

At the rear of the building, central balconies protruded from each of the three levels, separated by single brick partitions. Bugs crept to the back corner of the wall nearest the driveway, his eyes peeled for the security camera. He spotted it mounted above the double roller doors, pointing down at the driveway and entrance to the basement parking.

Good, I'll be in its blind spot.

Climbing onto the ground floor balcony, he balanced himself on the cast iron railing and then leapt up, grabbing hold of the railing on the second level balcony. Kicking off from the back wall, he was up and over an instant later. After putting an ear to the door and hearing no sounds from inside the unit, he jimmied open the back sliding door and disappeared inside.

Finding himself in a small living area, he moved swiftly and silently, checking each room, before moving on to the next apartment on that level. At first surprised to find none of the unit doors locked, he realised that made sense if the whole building were being used as a base. When he reached the top floor he found the internal wall between the two front apartments had been removed, effectively combining them into one large space. The place was clean, apart from a stack of dishes in the sink and a bin overflowing with pizza boxes.

And not a single person anywhere.

———

To counteract the sedentary nature of their work driving haul trucks and operating loaders, Modeen and Wolf made visits to the gym a daily routine whenever possible. The Mount Lester Mining Company had gone to some trouble and expense to provide good quality, commercial grade gym equipment in the recreation centre. According to the brochure in their induction packs, this was to 'assist in ensuring our workers' health and wellbeing'.

The gym room was air-conditioned, like most other places on site, and its thick blue industrial-grade carpet provided a comfortable, cushioned surface for floor exercises and stretches. Floor-to-ceiling mirrors covered one wall, while an assortment of purpose-built work stations, bench presses, treadmills, and a fully stocked dumbbell rack lined the other three. It wasn't a bad place to work out, so Modeen and Wolf were surprised to often find themselves the only ones there.

Their lightweight workout gear stuck to them as they jogged to the recreation centre that morning, taking advantage of the free time before their after-noon shift commenced. Slowing to a walk they entered the building next to the pool, as a white Toyota wagon covered in red dust pulled into the centre's carpark. Its four occupants sat silently inside, an inexplicable air of malice about them as they stared through the windows as though taking in the sights.

Inside the gym, Modeen and Wolf started their routines as usual by warming up on the treadmills. At the sound of heavy clunks coming from a weight stack, they glanced over to see one of the young blokes from nightshift working out on the multi-station. His jerky movements were compounded by the overly heavy weight setting on the station. If he hadn't done so already, he was going to do himself an injury.

Modeen winced and indicated for Wolf to inter-vene. He responded with a roll of eyes and a 'do I have to?' grimace, but was already making his way to the multi-station. The young bloke threw him a questioning frown which, when Wolf tried to give him a few pointers on technique, turned into a scowl.

'Look, mate,' he ground out, 'if I wanted your help I would've *asked* for it.' As he got off the station, Modeen saw a spasm of pain shoot across his face.

Too late. He'd already hurt himself.

Offended and embarrassed, the young man stormed out, clearly favouring his right side.

Wolf made his way back to the treadmill, shaking his head and grumbling, 'Young blokes. Can't tell 'em anythin'.'

Modeen threw him an apologetic look. 'Well, at least you tried. And better coming from you than from me.'

Stepping back onto the treadmill about to continue his warm-up, Wolf heard the door of the gym open again and then quickly close. Thinking the young bloke might've had second thoughts, he glanced over … and did a double take. Jumping off his machine, he reached over to hit the red panic button on Modeen's treadmill. She didn't wait for it to wind down to a full stop before springing off and following Wolf's gaze to the entrance.

A grey-bearded biker in a worn leather jacket sporting club colours, and armed with a compact nine millimetre Uzi, took up guard position at the door, while two Asian men moved into the clear area at the front of the room. Modeen recognised one of them from the attack in Melbourne. He had those damn titanium blue throwing knives strapped to his thighs. Removing two from their scabbards, he twirled them in his hands. Challenge glittered in his slanted eyes as he took up a defensive stance.

The other Asian slipped off his shirt, revealing an ornate dragon tattoo covering his entire back. He tossed the shirt at the feet of the biker and kicked off his shoes. Wearing loose-fitting long cotton pants cinched at the waist with a black belt, he tugged on the ends of the fabric belt to flatten the knot and turned to face Wolf and Modeen, holding out a metal tube. When he clicked the release mechanism, the tube extended into a martial arts long stick almost two metres in length.

Sweeping a glance around the room, Modeen spotted a wooden-handled broom amid an assortment of janitorial cleaning gear stacked in the nearest corner. The two Asians waited, their lips twisted in insolent sneers, while she grabbed the broom. Placing a foot on the brush head, she twisted off the handle. As she took up position in front of the man with the long stick, she set the broom handle into a rapid twirling motion using a figure eight cross-over technique. Beside her, Wolf faced off with the other man, dodging left to right and blocking the man's lunges and swipes with the gleaming blue blades.

Pirouetting and holding the broom handle by one end, Modeen lunged forward and swung it in a wide arc toward the man with the dragon tattoo. He ducked and stepped backward, but he wasn't the intended target. She completed the swing, cracking the man with the titanium blades squarely in the back of the head. As he fell forward, Wolf stepped in and followed through with a knee to the man's face. He collapsed to the floor as Wolf lifted a knife from his scabbard. Spinning one-eighty degrees in one fluid motion, Wolf launched the weapon at the throat of the biker by the door. The man dropped the Uzi and slid down the wall to the floor, both hands at his haemorrhaging throat.

Wolf bent to pick up the other two blades lying next to his now unconscious opponent, only to dive sideways when the man with the long stick stepped forward, swinging the weapon at his head. There was another crack as Modeen flew between them, deflecting the blow with one end of the broom handle, and then spinning and whacking the other end across the Asian's shoulder and neck.

In a flurry of metal clanking against wood they spun and danced, warding off each other's blows, until the man with the dragon tattoo leapt into the air, bringing down the metal long stick in a forward arc. With a splintering crack, Modeen's broomstick was snapped in two. She sprang back, now armed with a short, jagged stick in each hand.

Crack … crack … crack!

She warded off another volley of blows as Wolf yelled, 'Oi!' Holding one of the blue blades back and above his head, he lobbed it at the Asian, scowling as metal clanked against metal.

As the deflected knife clanged uselessly to the floor, Modeen lunged forward. In a double bluff attack, she held one stick high above her head as if to deliver a knockout blow while keeping her other arm tucked against her body. When he lifted his long stick to counter the high blow she whipped her other hand downward, and with a backhand throw, speared the stick into his shin. He gave a cry of pain and grimaced, barely managing to block the high thrust as she brought her other arm down. But his block wobbled as he gave a choked sound and slumped to the carpet.

Seeing the blue knife buried in the side of his neck, Modeen gave Wolf an approving nod as she moved to squat beside the biker's bloody body. After checking his pockets she rolled him over, taking the wallet from the back of his pants and rifling through it. When Wolf joined her, she held out a business card and then took a double take when she saw what he was wearing. Indicating the belt he'd donned, its scabbard now holding three of the blue throwing knives, she shook her head and raised an enquiring eyebrow at him.

Taking the card from her, he barked, 'What?' and then grinned sheepishly. 'He doesn't need the knives now. Besides, they're really well balanced.' As he spoke he bent to remove the remaining knife from the biker's throat, wiped the blade on the dead man's jacket, and slipped it into the scabbard.

Modeen collected the Uzi. Pulling back the slide, she clicked her tongue.

'What now?'

She gave a bemused huff. 'This guy was an amateur, it wasn't even loaded.'

'Oh.' Wolf looked disconcerted. 'I didn't know that.'

'You did good. As far as we knew, it *was* loaded.' Rising, she palmed home the magazine, released the slide and watched as the first bullet loaded into the breach. 'I guess it's not safe to hang around here.'

'Agreed.' Wolf studied the business card. 'I guess we should check out the Weipa biker's club.'

Thumbing the safety forward on the Uzi, Modeen peered through the glass door and murmured, 'Sentry … at the corner of the corridor. Another biker … may be armed.' She stared out at him. His back was turned and he was dragging on a cigarette.

Opening the door carefully and staying low, she crept up on the guard with Wolf close behind her.

Thrusting the muzzle of the Uzi into the side of the guard's neck she hissed, 'Don't move.'

The man jerked and then froze. Modeen kept the weapon pressed against his neck while Wolf patted him down. Tattoos covered every inch of his exposed skin, even his shaved head. Pulling a set of keys from the man's leather vest, Wolf jingled them at Modeen.

'Right. Let's go.' She nudged the guard in the back and they escorted him to the carpark, and the lone Toyota wagon waiting there.

CHAPTER TWELVE

When the biker's face thumped against the back door of the Toyota wagon, Wolf drawled, 'Sorry dude,' in mock apology. Grabbing a fistful of leather at the man's neck, he held him aside while opening the door and then shoved him head-first onto the back seat. With a quick glance around to see if anyone was watching, Wolf followed him inside and closed the door.

Modeen skirted around the back of the vehicle, taking care to keep the Uzi out of sight, and slid into the back seat on the other side of their captive.

Holding one of the wicked blue knives in front of the biker's face and twirling it expertly in one large hand, Wolf growled, 'You've got some fast talkin' to do, if you wanna stay in one piece.'

When the biker recoiled, Modeen pushed the muzzle of the Uzi into his side, making him gasp. Gritting his teeth, he ground out, 'You're wastin' your time. I don't know nothin'.'

Modeen shook her head slowly from side to side and clicked her tongue. 'Wrong answer.' She leaned on the Uzi, forcing the muzzle deeper into his bulk.

Throwing her a wink, Wolf said with fake regret, 'Don't think he's listenin'.' Then his tone brightened. 'So how about we start with an ear?' Moving the blade to the side of the man's temple, Wolf grabbed that ear with his free hand, drawling ominously, 'I'll stop cuttin' when you start talkin'.'

Feeling the chill of the knife's blade and the sting of its sharp edge rasping against his cheek, the biker's eyes widened. 'I t-told ya,' he pleaded, 'I don't know why they're after ya. I'm just the hired hand.'

Modeen prodded him with the Uzi. 'Who's "they"?'

'This … this Russian m-mob. They moved onto our turf and are throwin' their weight around.' His lips twisted and he added sourly, 'Been gettin' us to do their dirty work but keepin' us in the dark. Expectin' us to be bodyguards one minute 'n babysitters the next….'

Modeen frowned. 'Babysitters?'

'Yeah, we're helpin' keep an eye on some woman they're holdin'.' He scowled. 'Course they didn't tell us *why* they're holdin' 'er, 'n they don't like it when we ask questions … tell us we're just the muscle not the brains of the operation. 'N before y'ask, I dunno who she is.'

Wolf and Modeen exchanged a meaningful glance. Releasing the now talkative biker's ear, Wolf barked, 'So what *do* you know about this woman?'

'Nothin', 'cept that she looks like a classy lady, 'n they've got 'er at Mapoon.'

'Where the hell is Mapoon?'

Modeen caught Wolf's eye. 'North of Weipa, very remote.'

He nodded and addressed the biker again. 'Where in Mapoon is she being held?'

The man narrowed his eyes. 'What's that got to do with you?' When Wolf raised the knife again, he put his hands up in surrender. 'OK, OK. She's at the club's bush shack … off the Weipa to Mapoon Road.'

Modeen and Wolf nodded to each other. 'Right,' she announced, 'we're going for a ride.' She prodded the biker again, 'And you're coming with us. Behave and you'll get through this alive and in one piece.' With the Uzi still trained on him, she backed out of the Toyota and ordered, 'Get into the front.' She opened the front passenger's door and watched as he changed seats.

Wolf got behind the wheel while Modeen slid into the back seat again, directly behind the biker. As a reminder, she pressed the Uzi into the top of his shoulder while saying to Wolf, 'Stop at our place first. I'll keep him covered while you get the tactical gear. Don't forget to grab Walt for me.'

As they pulled out of the carpark, Modeen saw

some men in the swimming pool compound standing against the weld-mesh fence gazing at them.

Frowning, she said under her breath, 'Seems our altercation hasn't gone unnoticed.' She glanced at Wolf. 'I'll call it in.'

He gave a snort and drawled, 'We're outsiders now, remember.'

She shrugged. 'Right now it doesn't feel like we are. And we need to find out if Ben knows anything about this woman.'

Wolf gave a nod and focused his attention on the road.

When her caller ID popped up on his phone, Ben's expression lifted. 'JD,' he answered warmly, leaning back in his office chair, 'to what do I owe this pleasure?'

'Wolf and I just had some unwelcome visitors, and we recognised one as the Asian who tried to take us out in Melbourne.'

Ben sat upright and said with new urgency, 'You both OK?'

'We're fine.'

'How's Wolf holding up?'

'He's good. And here's a piece of news you might know something about. The people after us are also holding a woman captive. One of the goons described her as "classy".'

'Classy?'

'That's what he said.'

There was a pause and then Ben barked, 'Where is she being held?'

'In Mapoon, north of Weipa.'

'And you believe she's a hostage?'

'We assume so.'

'Right. I'll arrange to send some—'

Modeen cut him off. 'Wolf and I are heading there now so don't bother sending anyone. We'll handle it.'

'Look, JD, this could be related to a top priority mission the agency is currently involved in.'

'I understand, Ben, but they've made this personal by targeting us.' Modeen heard him sigh and could imagine him running through various scenarios in his head. She knew distance and travel time would factor greatly in all of them.

Seconds ticked by before he said, 'If this woman is who I think she could be, I need to know she's alive and safe, ASAP.'

'Roger. We'll keep you posted.'

'Are you armed?'

'Yep.'

'Stay sharp, this new faction's hard-core. Now, do you need anything?'

'We could use a cleaner at the gym in Lester's recreation centre.'

Ben gave a resigned sigh. 'How many bodies?'

'Three.'

He sighed again. 'That'll take some explaining.' After a loaded pause he added, 'You know … things would be a lot easier if you two were still with the agency.'

'Acknowledged. And thanks Ben.' When she ended the call, Modeen noticed the biker frowning incredulously at her and Wolf.

Finally he burst out, 'Who the hell *are* you guys?'

————

After noticing Brent and Spooky high-five each other as they completed the final mods and checks of the laser, Morris instructed them to go home for dinner. His tone was more moderate when he added, 'It's gonna be a long night.'

Spooky eyed him. Recalling Ben's orders to not let Morris out of his sight, he said brightly, 'I'm fine to carry on.'

Brent nodded. 'Me too. And we need to test the gen-set before the transport gets here.'

Instead of looking pleased with his co-workers' dedication, Morris frowned. 'Don't worry about the gen-set for now. You guys should take a break and get some rest.'

The last word was barely out of his mouth when Spooky chipped in, 'Brent's right, we should check the gen-set.'

Morris' expression darkened. 'It's a brand new

unit, guys,' he snapped, 'and it had to pass some pretty rigorous testing before being approved for delivery.' He put his hands on his hips. 'So go and take that break. The transport is due at twenty-one thirty, so we've still got a couple of hours before it arrives.'

Spooky was trying to come up with a plausible reason to hang around when Brent piped up, 'Hey, I feel like pizza. How about I order some in and we can *all* take a break?'

Quickly tugging a ten dollar note out of a pocket in his jeans, a grinning Spooky announced, 'Great idea! Make mine a BBQ meatlovers.'

Brent nodded. 'I'm havin' a Hawaiian. What about you, Phil?'

Morris stared at them and then said grudgingly, 'Guess I'll have the Godfather ... and a cola.'

With a distracted murmur of acknowledgement, Brent phoned in the order.

———

Without another vehicle within cooee, the Toyota wagon headed north out of Weipa on Andoom Road. As they approached the long, single-lane bridge over Mission River at Rocky Point, Modeen instructed Wolf to pull over. The network signal on her mobile phone had reduced to one bar and was likely to drop out altogether. As the car slid to a stop in the gravel on the side of the road, she held her phone forward for the biker to see the map on screen.

'Where *exactly* in Mapoon is this bush shack?'

The biker threw her a dirty look and then stared at the screen. Using two fingers to zoom in on some dwellings along the bank of the Wenlock River Inlet, he muttered, 'Here,' and tapped a spot on the screen. 'It's the first one in this line of shacks.'

Pulling her arm back, Modeen stared at the spot and zoomed the image in and out, pondering their plan of attack. 'I'd better contact Ben from here,' she murmured to Wolf, 'while we still have signal.' Opening the car door, she indicated the biker with a lift of her chin.

Wolf nodded. 'I'll watch him.'

After exiting the Toyota, Modeen walked a short distance behind it. She didn't want the biker to over-hear the conversation, even if it were a one-sided version.

'JD, report.'

'The hostage is being held in Mapoon, approxi-mately ninety minutes north of Weipa. It's a remote area, we'll likely be out of communication range soon. And out for about five hours.'

'Understood. Look, it's a long shot, but I'm sending you a photo of Susan Morris. If she *is* the woman being held there, I need to know ASAP.'

When her phone chimed with an incoming message, Modeen opened the jpg file attached and maximised the smiling image of a fifty-something, smartly dressed woman. Murmuring, 'Hold on, Ben,' she strode back to the car. Tapping on the passenger's side window to get the biker's attention, she held up the phone. 'Is this the woman?'

He squinted at the screen, saying nothing until Wolf prodded him in the side. Wincing, he gave a hasty nod.

Modeen turned and moved away again, once more putting the phone to her ear. 'We have a positive ID,' and she glanced back at the car, 'albeit from a reluctant source.'

'Your captive was able to confirm Susan Morris is the woman being held?' Ben's disbelieving tone was tinged with hope.

'Yes. We've yet to see her for ourselves of course.'

'Well, it sounds promising. Look JD, it's *imperative* Susan Morris stays alive and safe. Let me know when you have her secured, and above all, be careful.'

'Roger.' Modeen was already striding back to the waiting Toyota. Climbing into the back seat again, she nodded to Wolf. 'Let's go.'

He accelerated back onto the highway toward Mapoon. The Toyota kicked up a cloud of red dust after crossing the Mission River bridge where the road turned to gravel. Wolf switched on the headlights and decreased speed, aware nocturnal wildlife would be stirring in the fading dusk light. Wallabies were a well known hazard on outback roads, and hitting a large one could disable a vehicle, something they couldn't afford to have happen.

After a rough ninety minutes on the wide, corrugated gravel road the biker announced gruffly, 'Keep goin'. The turn-off's on the right, just past the Mapoon airfield.'

Five minutes later they passed a wide expanse of gravel on the left.

When Wolf barked, 'Is that the airstrip?' the biker muttered, 'Yep. Slow down, that's the turn-off comin' up.'

Ahead of them a narrow gravel track branched off the highway at a forty-five degree angle, to wind behind a thick forest of eucalypt trees. As they turned onto it Modeen leaned forward and instructed, 'Pull in anywhere along here, Wolf, and we'll conceal the car.'

'No!' the biker said abruptly. 'Follow the track to the end. There's a long driveway off to the right that leads to the shack.'

Ignoring the biker's urging, Wolf pulled off the road. Leaves and branches scraped against the white duco as he nosed the car into the vegetation, stopping behind some densely foliaged bushes that provided a screen from the track.

Minutes later, dressed in tactical night ops gear, he and Modeen set off through the bush, dogged for a short distance by the muffled protests of the biker they'd left bound and gagged behind. Pulling down her night-vision goggles and guided by the GPS app on her phone, Modeen led the way with Wolf close behind on her left. The thick undergrowth made progress slow. As they neared their target, she caught the smell of salt on the air and the rushing sound of waves against rocks.

About to throw Wolf a nod, she heard heavy pounding coming toward them from the bush ahead. Something was approaching ... rapidly. With a hasty hand signal to Wolf, she dropped to the ground and pulled the Walther PPQ from her shoulder holster. A few metres away, Wolf squatted and raised his Heckler and Koch G36 assault rifle. Using its Zeus thermal imaging scope to scan ahead, he saw two compact heat signatures parting the scrub like a bow wave and coming directly at him.

Hearing a low growl, Modeen readied herself for an attack as dark shapes sprang from the bushes. Wolf's assault rifle discharged twice in quick succession, its thick silencer muting each shot to a dull hiss. Modeen heard and felt two heavy thuds on the ground followed by some sliding sounds, and then an eerie silence settled. Rising, she hurried to Wolf's side. Two huge Rottweilers lay at his feet, one with trails of saliva oozing from its slack mouth while its glassy-eyed companion still had its vicious teeth bared.

He grunted. 'Guard dogs. The place'll be on alert once they're missed.'

Modeen nodded. 'C'mon. The shack should only be another fifty metres ahead.'

They'd only gone a short distance when a powerful flashlight beam cut through the bush, searching from side to side. As they ducked under cover, Wolf heard a man's voice calling, 'Come … COME,' in a thick foreign accent. Giving Modeen the signal to stay Wolf squatted, steadying an elbow against his bent knee. Once more raising the G36, he located the owner of the voice through the thermal scope.

Carrying a torch in one hand and an A-91 compact assault rifle in the other, the heavily-built man was pushing his way through the scrub toward them.

Now poised and motionless, Wolf put the cross hairs in the centre of the man's upper torso and squeezed the trigger. He watched through the scope as the armed man dropped to the ground. Breaking cover, Wolf moved cautiously to the fallen man's side and bent to check for a pulse. When Modeen joined him, he straightened and gave a thumbs down signal. She inclined her head without speaking and they continued moving forward.

Coming to a stop at the edge of a clearing a short time later, and silently congratulating her GPS's accuracy, Modeen stared at the large, green, corrugated shed approximately fifteen metres from their position. Harsh fluorescent lighting illuminated the interior of the building, and a hurricane lamp hung from the near side of a low veranda that extended along the shed's full length.

Beside her, Wolf peered through the thermal imaging scope and whispered, 'Four males, at a table on the western end.' And a moment later, 'Eastern side, one female against the back wall.'

With a decisive nod, Modeen fitted a silencer to her Walther PPQ and, keeping low, inched into the clearing.

CHAPTER THIRTEEN

Feeling Wolf grasp her shoulder, Modeen turned swiftly and saw him beckoning her to drop back. They crouched under cover as a man appeared from the corner of the shed. After executing a military-styled turn, he proceeded to patrol the full length of the veranda.

Wolf leaned in close to Modeen and whispered, 'Make that five males.'

Halting at the end of the veranda closest to them, the sentry spun on his heels and walked back to the front of the shed, calling, 'Mikhail! Mikhail! *Gde ty?'* then in English, 'Vere are you, Mikhail?'

Another man sauntered out to stand by the sentry's side and joined him in peering into the darkness.

When the sentry called again, 'Mikhail!' and once more received no response, the second man thumped him on the shoulder and ordered, *'Idti,'* before going back inside.

Obeying the order to go, the sentry pulled back the slide of his A-91, clicked the safety lever down, and stepped off the veranda to head into the bush.

Keeping low and moving silently in the dark, Wolf left Modeen's side, intent on intercepting the sentry. When he vanished into the scrub, she skirted around the trees to the far side of the clearing, where it was darkest. Approaching the shed from that side, she crept along the back wall to the edge of the veranda, only to flatten herself against the wall when Wolf rasped over the comms, 'Stand fast!'

The guard he'd spotted came out the front door of the shed. The man slung his weapon, walked to the corner and then started down the veranda.

Keeping his voice down Wolf said urgently, 'Guard coming your way. Armed, AK47.'

From her position against the wall Modeen pulled her night vision goggles down around her neck. Carefully raising her right foot, she reached down and slipped her combat knife from the scabbard strapped to her calf. Straightening and pressing herself against the wall, she held her breath when the guard came to a stop at the edge of the veranda near her.

He stood there briefly, clearing his throat and spitting a glob of phlegm onto the ground, before turning to retrace his steps.

Springing from the shadows, Modeen came at him

from behind. When she reached around to cover his mouth with her left hand he jerked, startled by the surprise attack. At around six foot in height, he was an inch taller than her, solidly built and muscular, so she couldn't afford to cut him any slack. Reefing his head back and to the left, she reached her knife hand up around his neck and dragged the razor-sharp blade across his throat in one swift movement. Muting his bellow with her hand, she tightened her hold on him as he clutched desperately at his throat, his body rigid with shock and fear. When his legs crumpled beneath him, she took the weight of his upper body and lowered him, gurgling and wheezing, to the ground.

His legs spasmed and he gave a final kick as she dragged him off the veranda. Once they were in the shadows, she squatted beside his now limp body to check he was no longer a threat, and wiped the blade of her knife across the front of his shirt. Returning it to the scabbard, she crept back to the corner and made her way down the veranda, hugging the shed wall.

Stopping at the corner of the first window she risked a look inside and saw three men, two of them leather-vested bikers, milling around the front door.

They were loading weapons.

Crouching low again, she crossed over to look through the other corner of the window. When she raised her head, she saw another man sitting on a bed in the room's back corner. He had a pistol – a Russian

Tokarev if she wasn't mistaken – pressed against a woman's temple.

Susan Morris's temple.

Suddenly the man's head whipped around as though he'd sensed Modeen's presence.

She dived to the floor as a volley of bullets exploded the window, showering her in shards of glass. When the second volley peppered bullet holes through the thinly-clad wall above her head, she scarpered to the front edge of the wall. Seeing the muzzle of an AK47 emerging from around the corner, she grabbed it with one hand and yanked it past her.

It was followed by one of the bikers. He froze and dropped the weapon as Modeen thrust the blade of her combat knife upward, through the soft tissue behind his chin, and into his skull. His eyes rolled back in his head as his body went limp. She pushed him aside as he crumpled to the floor, and reached for her Walther PPQ.

About to move, she took a step back as another guard dropped to the floor at the biker's feet with a neat entry hole in his forehead.

Troy hasn't lost his touch.

Just then his gravelly voice came over the comms. 'One to your right, unarmed. I've got you covered.'

'Copy that.' Seeing the last of the bikers standing just outside the door, his assault rifle on the ground in front of him and his hands behind his head in surrender, Modeen strode over to him and checked him for any additional weapons. Grabbing his tattooed arm and pressing the pistol into the side of his neck, she spun him around and marched him back into the shed.

At their approach the man inside yanked a whimpering Susan Morris to her feet. He took position behind her, one arm holding her quaking body against his and the other hand holding the Tokarev to her temple.

Modeen ordered, *'Opusti pistolet!'* Then in English. 'Put the gun down.'

The man peered around his captive's head at her. 'So, ze voman!' His eyes roved over her and he licked his lips. 'So we finally get to meet. Please to take off ze balaclava so I can see your face.'

Ignoring his request, she snapped, 'A prisoner for a prisoner.'

He gave a guttural laugh and in a blur of motion, raised his pistol and fired. Modeen ducked behind the biker. As his body slumped to the floor, she lifted her weapon to return fire, only to see the Russian's gun once more pressed against a sobbing Susan's head.

Using her as a shield, the Russian tucked his head behind hers and laughed again. The harsh sound grated down Modeen's spine.

'So, voman, vhat prisoner are you offering in return for zis one?' and he jabbed a finger into Susan's ribs, making her squirm.

Modeen stayed where she was, gripping the PPQ in both hands in readiness. 'Let her go.'

The Russian raised a lazy eyebrow and indicated the open doorway with a lift of his chin. 'I sink your friend should join us. Tell him to put down ze weapon and come inside.'

'I am alone.'

He grinned wickedly, showing uneven teeth. 'I don't sink so.' His pistol flicked forward again to aim at Modeen's chest. 'Now, drop your veapon and tell your friend to come in, or I vill shoot the both of y—'

The man's threat was cut short by a faint hiss from outside the window to Modeen's right. In front of her the Russian's head snapped sideways and his arms flew up as he staggered backward, the gun slipping from his grasp as he crashed to the floor. Finding herself suddenly freed, his open-mouthed captive lurched as if about to join him on the floor. Modeen hurried to catch her as she fainted.

Behind them, Wolf stepped through the side window, barking, 'You OK?'

At Modeen's nod, he made a swift search of the premises. When he returned he found Susan Morris on the floor, a rolled-up blanket cushioning her head and another covering her body. Modeen was nearby, bent over the dead Russian and going through his pockets.

'Toyota Hilux dual cab parked out front. No—' As he spoke, Modeen tossed him a set of keys and he gave a satisfied grunt. Then he gazed down at Susan Morris. 'She alright?'

'Just fainted as far as I can tell.' Modeen glanced up at him. 'Bring the car around?'

'Sure.'

Skidding the vehicle to a stop in front of the shed, Wolf lifted the oblivious Morris as if she weighed nothing and carried her to the Hilux. He lay her on the back seat while Modeen placed the rolled-up blanket under her head and covered her body with the other. Climbing into the driver's seat, Wolf started the engine and they tracked down the driveway and back to where they'd left the Toyota wagon concealed in the bush. Leaving the Hilux running, he jumped out and found the biker still secured in the back of the wagon. From the welts on his wrists the man had been testing the strength of his bonds.

Throwing him a narrow-eyed, knowing look, Wolf cut the wire ties with one of the blue blades and dragged him, stumbling, out of the wagon. As soon as the man regained his footing Wolf put the tip of the knife to his throat and growled, 'I ought'a stick you for not tellin' us about the dogs.'

The biker blanched. 'D-dogs?' he wheedled, 'I didn't know about any dogs.' When Wolf increased the upward pressure on the blade, the biker raised his voice. 'I didn't *know* I tell you! I tell you I DIDN'T KNOW!'

Wolf twisted his top lip in a snarl and shoved the

biker backward into the scrub. The man fell heavily into a thorny bush, gave a grunt of pain, and clutched at his shoulder. Pausing, Wolf eyed the wagon before climbing back into the Hilux. As he gunned it toward the main road, showering the biker in gravel and red dust in their wake, he gave a satisfied smirk.

Modeen flicked him a glance. 'Generous of you to leave him the wagon.'

'Not really.' Wolf's smirk widened as he buzzed down his window. Pulling the wagon's keys from a pocket in his cargo pants, he tossed them into the darkness with a casual flick of his wrist.

In the back seat, Susan Morris's eyes blinked open. She sucked in a breath and took stock of her surroundings before croaking, 'My husband.'

Hearing her, Modeen looked around.

'I need … to contact my husband,' Susan choked, 'let him know I'm alright. His name's Philip Morris … he's in Nowra.'

'It's OK, Susan,' Modeen soothed, 'you're safe with us. And your husband …' She glanced at Wolf who raised expressive eyebrows but said nothing. 'The authorities know of his situation.'

Seeing Susan sigh and close her eyes, Modeen said, 'Rest now. We'll talk some more when you feel up to it.'

· · ·

At twenty-three fifty they were back on the other side of Mission River bridge at Rocky Point, when Modeen's phone buzzed and vibrated with incoming messages. Murmuring, 'We're back in mobile network range,' she checked the messages and turned to Wolf. 'Pull over, I'd better give Ben a call.'

He answered on the second ring. The tense edge to his voice softened as she gave a rundown of events. 'Good work, JD. Now I know Susan Morris is alive and well, we have the advantage and can act accordingly.'

'What do you want us to do with her?'

'You've already done more than enough.' Ben gave a snort and added drily, 'Especially considering you're no longer sanctioned agents. That said, I still need you to keep her safe and out of harm's way, until I can organise someone to relieve you.'

After a nod from Wolf, Modeen replied, 'No problem, but can I make a suggestion?'

'Sure, what is it?'

'We could drop her off at Scherger RAAF base.'

'Scherger … just outside Weipa.' After a brief, thoughtful pause Ben announced crisply, 'Good idea. I'll make the arrangements now.'

He pressed End Call, intending to contact Scherger straightaway, only to realise he had a more urgent call to make. Tapping on Spooky's number, he pressed his lips together in frustration when his unanswered call went to voice mail.

CHAPTER FOURTEEN

A thunderous roar filled the cargo hold. Spooky, Morris and Brent were thrown back in their seats as the four powerful Pratt and Whitney Turbofan engines propelled the C17 Globemaster down the main runaway of HMAS Albatross base. Once airborne, the giant transport plane, on loan for the laser project from Air Mobility Command out of Travis AFB, California, and one of over two hundred C17s built for the US military, banked left and climbed to thirty thousand feet, bound for Woomera base.

In addition to the three Advanced Laser Optics representatives, the plane carried a minimal crew of pilot, co-pilot, and loadmaster. With the Oshkosh securely locked down in the centre of its twenty-seven metre long belly, the Globemaster levelled off and settled into its cruising speed of four hundred and fifty knots.

The three passengers sat without speaking. It was difficult to hear anything over the rumble of large jet engines, airframe vibrations and squeaks, and the buffeting of outside air against the cargo hold. When Spooky felt movement in his top pocket, he checked his phone and saw an incoming call from Ben. From the Call Log, it appeared he'd missed two of Ben's previous calls.

Muttering, 'Damn,' he pressed Answer and cupped a hand over his other ear to block some of the noise.

'Good news, Spook. Susan Morris is safe and secure.'

Spooky bent his head and pressed his hand and the phone firmer against his ears. 'That's great, Ben.'

'It's time to grill Morris,' Ben went on. 'Once he knows his wife is safe, he should be free to tell you what he knows about the attempt to steal the laser. Call me back ASAP when you have something.'

'Shall do.' As he shut down his phone, Spooky looked up.

Into the muzzle of an assault rifle.

The man holding it wore night ops gear and a parachute, as did the two standing in front of Morris and Brent. They kept their weapons trained on them as the man in front of Spooky stepped forward and pushed his rifle's muzzle into Spooky's forehead. Reefing the phone out of Spooky's hand, he dropped it to the floor and then crushed it under his combat boot.

With a guttural yell of, 'Hands up!' he jabbed the

muzzle into Spooky's forehead again. When Spooky complied, staying where he was and gazing levelly at him, the man looked away briefly. Spooky took the opportunity to glance sideways at Brent and Morris. They had their hands behind their heads, shocked eyes wide and fearful as one of the other men searched them.

The man in front of Spooky, the tallest of the three, barked orders at the other two in what sounded like Russian, before moving to the Oshkosh. The second Russian hurried toward the cockpit while the third stood guard over their three captives, every now and then glancing over his shoulder at the tall man, who was now at the Oshkosh. Spooky saw him push the front panel of the gen-set aside, drag out a drogue chute, and secure the chute to the rear ramp with a quit release hitch. He then returned to the gen-set and removed its outer shroud.

Watching him, Spooky shook his head as the shroud hit the floor. The whole interior of the gen-set had been gutted and a large cargo chute sat where the diesel motor should've been.

So that's how they got on board, by stowing away inside the gen-set.

He glanced at the exhaust stack and electrical couplings.

All fake. I should've realised….

Scowling, he bent his head, certain of what was about to happen.

Working swiftly, the Russian secured the cargo chute to the laser module at the front of the Oshkosh and released the holding clamps on both platforms. Satisfied all was in readiness, he returned to the front of the cargo bay and checked his mobile. When he barked, *'Tridtsat minut,'* at the man guarding them, Morris muttered, 'Thirty minutes,' for the benefit of his two colleagues. This earned him a muzzle jab in the chest and a bellow of, 'SILENCE!' from the guard.

What was taking so long? Surely Morris would blab now he knew his wife was safe?

Ben dialled Spooky's number again and when that call went to voice mail, tried once more a few minutes later.

Voice mail … again.

With a frustrated grunt, he sat back in his chair. The house, normally alive with sounds – clatter from the kitchen as Emily prepared their next meal, the buzz of music and voices from the TV, Chelsea's gurgles and cries as she woke from a nap – was still and silent. He checked his watch. It was just before midnight.

Rising, he made for the stairs and then stopped, knowing Emily would be sound asleep in their room. This was no time to be going to bed, anyway, there was too much happening, too much at stake. Turning, he went to the kitchen and switched on the kettle. While waiting for it to boil he checked the tracking app on his phone. On the screen Spooky, and the tracking device TD5685, moved swiftly across the centre of New South Wales. They were still in the air at least, and would soon be flying over Broken Hill.

Ben sniffed.

I'll give him another ten minutes.

The green hue from the avionics cathode ray screens, instrument clusters and heads-up display filled the cabin of the C17. The pilot scowled as the A-91 assault rifle prodded him in the shoulder, but he obediently eased the throttle back.

In the cargo hold Spooky heard the change to the engines' drone and felt the plane decrease speed. Nearby, the comms unit on the tall Russian's vest crackled and Spooky caught the murmur of Russian words, obviously from the second man in the cockpit.

With a curt, 'Da,' the tall Russian nodded at the third man still standing guard over the three captives, and then marched to the back of the jet. Spooky watched him secure himself to a lanyard before lowering the ramp. Once the ramp was down and locked in place, the man checked his phone once more.

When their guard looked away, Brent nudged Spooky and hissed, 'What's he doing?'

Spooky kept his voice low. 'Checking GPS coordinates I'd reckon.'

They watched the tall Russian wait for what felt

like an age but in reality was only a few minutes, and then he pulled the rip chord on the drogue chute secured to the centre of the floor. The chute rocketed outward into the darkness and opened, its small canopy twitching and weaving in the huge transport's slipstream.

Yelling, *'Idti! Idti!'* into his comms unit, the tall Russian yanked the quick release cord for the main chute. As he threw himself back against the fuselage wall, the drogue chute ripped the large cargo chute into the dark behind it. An instant later the laser module rocketed off the back of the Oshkosh.

And disappeared into the night.

The three captives stared out into the darkness after the precious cargo, but at the sound of rapid machine gun fire from the cockpit they whipped their heads around. As the jet's nose dipped, their guard threw them a triumphant grin. He backed away, still covering them with his weapon for a distance, before turning and jogging to the back of the plane. Following his tall comrade, he leapt off the ramp into the night sky.

Spooky had already unclipped his seatbelt as the last of the three Russians emerged from the cockpit and made for the ramp. Leaping to his feet, Spooky crash-tackled the man to the floor. Seeing that, Brent unclipped his belt with shaking fingers and stumbled forward, clawing his way along the bulkhead and into the cockpit. Once there he stopped dead, mouth agape.

All three crew members were dead, slumped over where they sat.

Glancing desperately at the control panels, Brent took in the shattered screens, exposed wiring, and bullet-ridden panels, all shot to hell. Then movement on the floor caught his eye as something rolled toward his feet.

The grenade's pin was missing.

Spooky had just knocked out the remaining Russian as the cockpit exploded, rocking the plane and blasting the cockpit door into the cargo bay. Ducking and throwing up an arm to shield his head, Spooky hurriedly stripped off the Russian's parachute. As he undid the buckles he glanced over at Morris. Still seated in the crash position, the cowering engineer had his face buried in his hands. Bellowing at him to get up, Spooky shrugged into the parachute harness and made his unsteady way toward Morris, who didn't move.

On reaching him, Spooky unceremoniously shoved him upright and unclipped his seatbelt. Grabbing him by the collar, he hauled the terrified man to his feet and marched him to the back of the plane.

'Wait!' Morris cried. 'What about Brent?'

'He's gone.'

'Gone?'

'Dead.'

Morris moved as though in a trance until he noticed the end of the ramp coming up fast. When he made to stop, Spooky changed his grip. Grasping the seat of Morris' pants with one hand and the back of his collar with the other, he ran forward, forcing a screaming Morris ahead of him and off the end of the ramp. As they tumbled into the darkness, an open-mouthed Morris turned to face Spooky, who wrapped his arms and legs around him.

Locked together, they fell, the roar of the jet's engines loud in their ears.

As the doomed aircraft continued its shallow dive toward the ground, Spooky tightened his hold on a gasping, whimpering Morris and pulled the drogue of his chute. After having the air knocked out of them by the initial force of the chute opening, Spooky relaxed his grip as Morris clamped his arms tighter around him.

With both hands now free to control the steering cords, Spooky searched the sky for signs of the parachuting Russians and stolen laser module. To his right the lights of a town – Broken Hill he figured – shone brightly up at them.

Then he stiffened as a distinctive sound reached his ears. It was the thump, thump, thump, of a Huey helicopter. Sweeping a glance around the darkness, he spotted the chopper passing below and to the left of them. He looked ahead of it, predicting its course, and made out a cluster of two huge cargo chutes some way in the distance.

That was where the chopper was headed.

Out of the corner of his eye he glimpsed a bright flash of light. Snapping his head around, he saw a fireball, like a glowing orange mushroom cloud, fill the horizon beyond Broken Hill. A deafening boom followed an instant later.

He shook his head sadly.

So much for the C17 and her crew.

Soon his every thought was fixed on trying to breathe. Morris was squeezing him like a boa constrictor. Even after they'd hit the ground, Spooky had to struggle free from Morris' vice-like grasp.

Whimpering, 'It wasn't supposed to happen like this,' Morris found his feet and finally released his hold on Spooky. 'They were just supposed to take the laser and leave us in peace.'

Spooky coughed, took some deep breaths, and then said sourly, 'That's the trouble with bad guys, Morris, you can't trust *anything* they say.' He began unstrapping the chute. 'Oh, and by the way, your wife has been rescued.'

'Susan's … safe?' Morris stared wide-eyed at him, his expression a mixture of hope and disbelief.

'Yes, she's safe.'

'You're sure about that?'

'I'm sure.'

Morris's voice increased in pitch. 'But how can you know?' His tone grew shrill. 'Who rescued her?' He was now almost shouting. 'Where is she—'

Fixing him with hard eyes Spooky barked, 'Pull

yourself together, Morris,' as he finished shrugging off the chute. 'We've got a long walk ahead of us.'

Morris stared at him. Even in his distressed state, he could tell their roles had been reversed. Luke was clearly now in charge and he, Morris, was the subordinate.

Ben swore under his breath.

Still no answer from Spooky.

Pulling out his phone he checked the tracking app again to confirm Spooky's location. West of Broken Hill … and stationary. How could that be when tracking device TD5685 – the one Spooky had planted on the laser – was still moving, heading north-east fast and directly across the desert?

Could the C17 have been hijacked … and Spooky thrown out?

Blinking and running an agitated hand over his head, Ben zoomed in on Spooky's location again.

Was he stationary or moving?

He stared at the blip.

It was moving. Slowly … but definitely moving.

Not realising he'd been holding his breath, Ben released it in a gush through pursed lips. He stared at the blip, pondering his next course of action.

One thing was for certain … this was going to be a long night.

At the abrupt vibration of his phone, he glanced at the screen before answering gruffly, 'Report, Bugs.'

'The convoy has turned off the Barrier Highway at Wilcannia, and is now on the Old Opal Mines Road, about twenty kilometres out of White Cliffs.'

'Hang on a second.' Ben searched for White Cliffs on his mobile's map. He found it, north-west of Broken Hill.

In the general direction of where the laser was heading.

He barked, 'Bugs!' but got no answer. 'Bugs, are you there?'

Barrelling along the narrow gravel road, Bugs was already struggling to see Craig's tail lights in the dust ahead when he was hit with the blinding glare of a spotlight from above. His ears caught the familiar thump, thump, thump of a Huey as his vehicle was engulfed in a hail of machine gun fire. He fought to keep control of the Aurion as both front and rear tyres on the passenger side blew. As he managed to slide the crippled vehicle to a stop in a cloud of dust, Bugs saw the chopper swoop low overhead and he caught the silhouette of a large rectangular object strapped to its belly.

His stomach clenched as he watched the Huey arch around and make for Craig's vehicle.

Hitting the boot release, Bugs leapt from the car,

raced to the rear and snatched up the M72 LAW, pre-packed with a standard anti-armour warhead. He yanked out the locking pin and slid the anti-tank weapon's back extension open and into the firing position, releasing the front and rear pop-up sights. As he sprinted through the settling dust, he raised the rocket launcher to stare through the bouncing open sights as the helicopter made its attack run.

He saw it swoop downward onto Craig's Aurion some two hundred meters ahead.

The chopper was right at the limit of the rocket launcher's effective range, but Bugs had no other option. He fired off the round, just as sparks flew from the muzzle of an M60 machine gun suspended from a gantry above the chopper's cargo bay. Bugs slid to a stop and held his breath as the rocket-propelled grenade streaked toward the chopper on an intercept course.

As though sensing the fast-approaching projectile, the chopper banked sharply and the grenade sailed harmlessly past it.

Bugs' shoulders slumped as he watched the chopper straighten and accelerate northward. Dropping his chin to his chest briefly, he lifted it again to jog toward where he'd last seen Craig's Aurion, dreading what he would find when he got there.

CHAPTER FIFTEEN

'Bugs!' Ben's shout issued from the mobile lying face-up amid the mound of takeaway coffee cups, screwed-up paper bags and crushed cans on the floor. The rubbish had provided a padded landing for the phone when Bugs dropped it while struggling to keep control of the damaged car. 'Bugs, pick up!' Hearing the thunk of the car's door and the scrape of denim on a leather seat followed by a grunt, Ben shouted again, 'Bugs, are you there?'

There were scrabbling sounds and then Bug's voice came on. 'Yeah Ben.' He sounded out of breath.

'You and Craig OK?'

'We are, thanks to the Aurion's armour plating. We got hit by a—'

'Huey,' Ben cut in. 'Yeah, I heard. It's been a while but there's no mistaking that sound. What did they hit you with?'

'M60 I'd reckon. Took out both the tyres so I'm not gonna be drivin' anywhere, anytime soon. Was wishin' I had a Stinger in the boot. Things would'a been different then.' Bugs swore under his breath. 'I took a shot at the Huey with the LAW … might've got it too if the chopper hadn't banked suddenly. Only missed by a few metres.'

'Well, I reckon you're the first agent to try and take down a chopper with an LAW72.' There was a grin in Ben's voice. 'They're not meant to be used as ground-to-air weapons.' His tone grew serious again. 'And in one way, it's good you missed. That Huey's carrying cargo a lot of important people want recovered intact.'

'I noticed a large crate strapped to its belly. The last I saw of it, the chopper was headin' north … but I'm guessin' you're not gonna be sendin' a Hornet after it?'

'You guess right. There's a tracker on the cargo, so we can at least follow where it goes for now.' At Bugs' grunt of acknowledgement Ben went on. 'How's Craig's car? Out of operation like yours?'

'She's a write-off, belly-up in a ditch. He got hit in the side like I did but ended up rollin' it.' Bugs gave an amused snort. ''N he's got the bruises to prove it. Anyway, we're thinkin' we might be able to swap the wheels around and make mine driveable.'

'Well, let me know how you get on. If you get it going you can rendezvous with Spook in Broken Hill. Otherwise, sit tight. The transport I'm organising to pick him up could collect you and Craig as well.'

'Is Spooky out here too?'

'Yes. On foot I believe, and heading for the Barrier Highway just outside Broken Hill. Anyway, keep me posted.'

'Copy that.'

As he hung up from that call Ben immediately made another. When Modeen answered, he barked, 'JD, are you and Wolf still at Scherger?'

'We just got here. Susan Morris is being put into protective custody as we speak.'

'Good work. Now, you still want to help?'

'Sure.'

'Right, I want you and Wolf to wait at the base. The situation has changed and I may need you to deploy on short notice.'

'Ready to go, Ben. Say, how long since you've been to Scherger?'

There was a long pause and then Ben said, 'Not sure … a long while. Why?'

'Well, the place is pretty run-down. Apparently the barracks were used as a refugee holding facility for a few years and got trashed by the inmates. There's only a skeleton crew here now, and I don't see anything in the way of aircraft. So if you're thinking of flying us out, you'll need to organise transportation from elsewhere.'

'Noted.' As Ben ended the call his phone vibrated with another one and the caller ID flashed on screen. It was NatSec Operations Manager Jack Pender. Ben gave a resigned sigh and pressed Answer.

Without preamble his boss barked, 'Ben, what do you know about a US Air Force C17 going down outside of Broken Hill?'

Ben took a moment to think and then said carefully, 'Not as much as you by the sounds of it.'

The calm tone in Ben's voice did nothing to relieve Jack's tension. 'I don't appreciate being woken up in the middle of the night,' he snapped, 'to be interrogated over something I know nothing about. The Yanks are demanding answers. They want to know how and why it crashed, and if the cargo was destroyed along with the aircraft.'

Ben heard him breathe out loudly.

When Jack spoke again his tone was calmer, though still business-like. 'I thought you had an agent with the cargo at all times?'

'I did,' Ben hastened to assure him, 'but I've lost communication with him.'

There was a brief, tension-charged silence on the line before Jack said brusquely, 'Look, Washington's making a lot of noise over this. I've got the Vice Chairman of the Joint Chiefs of Staff at the Pentagon breathing down my neck, not to mention our own PM who's also been contacted. Everyone's demanding answers. The Yanks have already dispatched one of their own crash investigators. It's midday over there now, and I've promised them a briefing by the time they sit down to dinner. So you'd better get moving.'

'Noted.'

'The RAAF has already been deployed to secure the scene.' With that, Jack ended the call.

Ben breathed out in a gush.

That went better than I expected. Lucky for me, Jack's a reasonable man.

Checking the tracking app on his phone again, he located the blip that was the Huey. It had crossed the New South Wales border into Queensland and was still tracking north. After making a few quick calls, Ben scratched a note on a piece of paper and made his way upstairs. Taking care to move quietly, he took the steps two at a time and then crept into the bedroom. Bending over the bed, he placed the note on Emily's bedside table and dropped a kiss on his sleeping wife's forehead.

Straightening, he collected the keys from his bedside table and returned downstairs. After making his way to the three bay garage, he opened the boot of his NatSec Aurion and scrutinised its contents. Taking out a black duffel containing night ops gear, he went to a metal two-door cabinet beside the workbench on the back wall of the garage. He flicked through the keys on his key ring and, selecting one, undid the padlock on the cabinet. Opening both doors, he reached a hand toward the back of the top shelf. When his searching fingers found the two levers he turned them, one clockwise and the other anti-clockwise. Hearing a solid clunk, he closed the doors again.

A set of heavy-duty hinges groaned as he swung the whole cabinet to one side, revealing a concealed walk-in armoury in the wall behind it. On the left, his old SASR camo M14 EBR tactical rifle headed a column of assault weapons, which included a pristine Barrett MRAD .388 sniper rifle in deep bronze. Along the back, M32 and XM25 grenade launchers, and a Matador rocket launcher, hung above a collection of grenades, C4 charges and detonators. On the right wall, a matched pair of two-tone CZ Shadow 2 pistols featured amid a variety of hand guns.

Duffel by his side, he stood contemplating his arsenal before taking a matt black Glock17 and four spare clips off the shelf. After slipping them into the bag, he bent to grab a pair of combat boots on his way out. Swinging the cabinet closed, he listened for the solid click of the locking mechanism before striding to the Aurion. After placing the boots and duffel on the car's back seat, he checked his app again.

The Huey was still on a northern heading, toward the Gulf of Carpentaria.

Ben slipped into the driver's seat and started the Aurion, wincing when the remote-controlled garage door gave a metal-on-metal squeal on opening. Telling himself to give it a good greasing when he got home he backed out slowly, doing his best to be quiet, and idled down the driveway. After turning onto the highway, he planted his foot on the accelerator and the big car leapt forward.

As he headed for Williams RAAF base at nearby Point Cook, an incoming call came through the car's Bluetooth speakers. He frowned, not recognising the number.

Stabbing a finger on the Answer button he said, 'Smith.'

'Ben, Spooky here. Look, the C17 is down and the cargo's been taken.'

'Yeah Spook, I've been tracking you and the cargo. I take it you're OK?'

'Yep, so's Morris.'

'Good. Report.'

'Three insurgents stowed away in the gen-set on the back of the Oshkosh. Once we were airborne they hijacked the plane and used cargo chutes to airdrop the module. Then they shot the crew and blew up the cockpit. I managed to get out with Morris in tow … which made for an interesting jump, I can tell you.' Spooky gave a wry snort.

'On the way down, I saw a Huey heading away with the package on board. From the smoke plume I'm guessing the C17 crashed about thirty kilometres north-east of Broken Hill. The two pilots and load master, along with Morris's 2IC, didn't make it.'

There was a loaded pause before Ben said gruffly, 'What does Morris have to say for himself? Anything useful about who we're up against or where they're taking the cargo?'

'Nah. He reckons his part was to swap out the gen-set prior to the last laser test. He never saw any of the people holding his wife hostage. The only communication he had with them was through the spy pens. They promised him no one would be injured and he'd get his wife back once they'd secured the module.'

When Ben muttered sourly, 'Great,' Spooky's tone lightened. 'Here's a piece of good news though. Morris tells me he built in a safeguard. Apparently the targeting software he loaded on the final test will render the laser useless. He also replaced one of the main circuit cards with a dummy, and says it'll take them months to make it work.'

'Well that's something at least.' Ben pulled onto the roadside and checked his tracking app. He could see Spooky's blip on the highway, approximately ten kilometres from Broken Hill. 'Who's phone are you using?'

'Some civic-minded local's. Luckily for us he let me flag him down on the highway and commandeer his mobile. He's gonna give us a lift into town.'

Ben gave a grunt followed by a thoughtful silence. Finally he said, 'Got your night ops gear with you?'

'Nah, didn't think I'd need it on the plane. And we had to bail out pronto so there wasn't time to grab anything 'cept a chute. What've you got in mind?'

'Drop off Morris at the Broken Hill police station,' Ben ordered. 'I'll let them know he's on the way. Once he's secure, get yourself to the airport and wait for me. I'll organise some kit for you. We'll go from there.'

'We? You coming out?'

'I am.' Ben ended the call and immediately dialled Bugs. 'Report.'

'Just finished changin' over the tyres,' Bugs puffed, and Ben heard him slapping a hand against his pants. 'Looks like we're mobile again so we'll make for Broken Hill.'

'Good work. Spook's on his way there too, with Morris.' Ben tapped on his mobile's screen. When he heard Bugs' phone ping with the incoming text he said, 'Call him on that number I just sent you. Arrange to pick him up at the police station, then head over to the airport and wait for me there.'

'Shall do. Say, you plannin' on joinin' us grunts in some field work?'

Ben gave a peeved snort and muttered, 'We're not in the Army anymore, mate. And yes, I am.' Stabbing the End Call button, he took another glance at his tracking app and noted the Huey's continuing northward course. Passing over Diamantina Lakes, it was making for Cloncurry, possibly Mount Isa. Putting the car in gear, Ben pulled back onto the road in a shower of gravel and continued toward the RAAF base. As he drove he scrolled through the contact list on the screen in the car's centre console and tapped on the number for NatSec Resource Manager Leanne Martin.

It took a few rings before his call was answered,

and when a sleepy voice breathed, 'Hello,' he looked at the digital clock on the Aurion's dash.

Still only two am.

Oh well, there's nothing else for it. And she knows being woken at all hours comes with the job.

'Sorry about the hour, Leanne, but I need you to make some urgent calls.' He heard the snap of a lamp being turned on, the crackle of note paper, and a stifled yawn.

A sleepy male voice said in the background, 'Wha? What's goin' on?'

Ben heard Leanne say, 'It's OK, sweetie, go back to sleep,' and then she spoke to him again, sounding more alert. 'Sure Ben, go ahead.'

Even for a major city like Melbourne, traffic at that time of the morning was light. Ben had just finished speaking to Leanne when he braked beside the security gate at the RAAF base. As the officer manning the gate approached the Aurion, Ben flashed his NatSec ID and received a nod.

He sat drumming his fingers on the steering wheel as the boom gate began to rise.

CHAPTER SIXTEEN

The eight-seater King Air's Pratt and Whitney turboprops gave the compact plane a maximum cruising speed of five hundred and seventy kilometres an hour. Quicker than any damn chopper, Ben decided. With a brusque, 'If that's the only plane ready to go, it'll have to do,' he moved to stand in front of the pilot.

The man looked up at him and, taking in his commanding presence, took a step back. Trying for an officious tone, he said, 'Williams Base is a training facility, and our King Air 350s are for VIP transport and cadet pilot training purposes only.'

Bending to look him in the eyes, Ben said with deceptive calmness, 'Time is critical and this is a top priority mission. Now do I have to wake up your group captain so you can discuss the matter with him, or should I call Canberra HQ direct?' He took out his mobile as he spoke.

Unnerved, the pilot shifted his feet and muttered resignedly, 'Meet me on the tarmac in ten,' before making his way from the briefing room.

Ben watched him go before changing into his night ops gear and heading out to the tarmac. Dropping his duffel at the plane's rear hatch he glanced over at the hangar.

No sign of the pilot or co-pilot yet.

He began pacing up and down, and then paused to check the time.

If these guys get their acts together we should be in Broken Hill in a little over an hour….

In the large, well-equipped but mostly empty kitchen on Scherger base, Modeen and Wolf managed to rustle up a simple meal. After watching her swallow the last remnants of toasted cheese and tomato sandwich, Wolf threw Modeen an amused look. Raising his coffee mug in a toast he drawled, 'Eat when you can, sleep when you die.'

They clanked cups and shared a wry grin, as Modeen's phone buzzed with an incoming call. She glanced at the screen and saw a familiar name.

'Hey Leanne, how's things?'

'Good thanks, Jo.' Leanne's tone was pleasant but businesslike. 'Hey, Ben asked me to keep you informed on developments.'

'Yep, so what's happening?'

'I've arranged for a Spartan to deploy to your location. It's coming from Townsville and should land at Scherger in just over an hour. We're not sure of the destination as yet, but the plane will be equipped with two HALO chutes and night ops gear just in case.'

'Copy that.'

'When we have an update, Ben or I will contact you with further instructions.'

'Roger.'

When Leanne ended the call, Modeen turned to meet Wolf's expectant gaze. 'They're sending a Spartan from Townsville, equipped with a couple of HALO chutes.'

With a shrug of broad shoulders, Wolf muttered, 'Great,' and gave a droll snort. 'I shouldn't have had that second helpin' of eggs.'

Moving closer, Modeen put her arms around him and pressed her lips against his tanned forehead. 'You're not having second thoughts about this, are you, Mr Ryan?'

His lips twitched and he shook his head. 'Not Ryan any more. We left our NatSec aliases behind when we resigned.' Pulling her onto his lap, he stared into her eyes. 'But I'm just…,' and he frowned. 'Just wonderin' if we'll ever be free of all this.'

She brushed an unruly lock of hair out of his eyes and said softly, 'It's still early days, Troy. It won't always be like this.' At his nod she went on firmly, 'Besides, I wasn't convinced that dropping off the radar and hiding out in a mining town out the back of Woop-Woop was the great start we needed. Although I have to hand it to Wolverton Station, we'd be hard-pressed to find a more remote place.'

Lifting her chin, she mused, 'Must be lucrative, having a multi-national mining company take a long term lease on a large chunk of property like that.' With a glint of mischief in her china-blue eyes, she nudged him. 'Are you sure you're not related to the owners? I mean … it's even spelled the same.'

Wolf gave a bark of laughter. 'I wish! But like I said, it's owned by the Jacksons.' He paused and then added, 'Ironic that Spooky's family, not mine, has connections to Wolverton Station … and lucky for us they did.' His fingers made a rasping sound as he rubbed his chin. 'We might've found it harder gettin' work at the mine if the Jacksons hadn't put in a good word for us.'

'So it's just coincidence the station shares your family name?'

''Fraid so.' A far-away look crept into his dark eyes. 'Y'know, when we first met after enlistin', Spooky told me about his family connection with Wolverton Station. I guess my havin' the same name as the station gave us somethin' in common. Anyway, it helped forge our friendship and led to my meetin' you.' Focusing on her again he gave a crooked smile. 'Wish I was your mega-rich lover,' he drawled, giving her a squeeze, 'but I'm afraid you're gonna have to settle for an ex-grunt slash agent slash rock ape.'

'And that's just fine by me.' She paused to kiss him before rising to her feet. 'Besides, as a decorated Special Forces soldier, you weren't an ordinary grunt.' She sobered. 'You're just the kind of man I need by my side, especially in encounters like those we've had recently.'

Wolf nodded. 'Think we were a bit lucky there. But at least we had the advantage of surprise which helped us reduce their numbers.' He gave a thoughtful frown. 'I'm not suggestin' we go back to NatSec full time, but maybe we should give some thought to Ben's suggestion about freelancin'? At least we could work together, and pick the missions that suit us.'

When Modeen dipped her head in agreement, he held up a fist and she leaned in to bump it with her own. Smiling into each other's eyes they recited together, 'Who dares wins!'

The sight of two large men dressed in black pants, skivvies and combat boots striding purposely through the front doors, had the night-duty officer at Broken Hill police station reaching for his sidearm.

'It's alright,' Spooky hastened to assure him, 'they're with me.'

Bugs flashed them a toothy grin while beside him Craig raised his hands as if in surrender. 'Easy there big fella,' Bugs said amiably to the officer, 'we're not armed.'

Taking his hand off his pistol, the chagrined officer muttered, 'Nothin' much normally ever happens around here at this time of the mornin', but it's been *crazy* the last half an hour. The phones've been running hot, what with the plane crash 'n all.'

Bugs and Craig raised their eyebrows at Spooky, but it was the police officer who answered when Craig enquired, 'Plane crash?'

'Yeah, a big one. About thirty clicks north-east of here.' He glanced at the wall clock. 'Emergency services should be there 'round about now.'

Spooky lifted his chin at Bugs and Craig. 'I'll fill you in on the way to the airport.' Then he addressed the officer. 'So you're right to look after Mr Morris?'

'Yep, got him tucked up nice 'n safe in one of the cells out the back.' The officer's good humour was returning. 'And I'll make sure he gets fed in the morning.'

Spooky nodded, 'Cheers, mate,' and joined Bugs and Craig who'd moved to the doorway. 'Right lads, lets get to the airport.'

Once outside, they made for the bullet-peppered Aurion.

Seeing it, Spooky gave a long whistle. 'You blokes have a rough trip here?'

The other two either ignored him or didn't hear,

their gazes fixed on a large orange glow on the horizon.

Bugs pointed toward it. 'That the plane?'

Spooky sighed. 'US Army C17.'

Bugs winced and shook his head. 'Oh man, the Yanks are gonna be pissed.'

Spooky gave a grunt of agreement.

'And I'm guessin',' Bugs went on, keeping his voice low, 'the crate strapped to the undercarriage of the Huey we ran into contained the laser module?'

'Correct.'

'And Ben's trackin' it, right?'

'Yeah.' Spooky paused to check his watch. 'We're to meet him at the airport. He should be there in fifteen.'

After Bugs steered the Aurion into the visitors' car park and nosed into a bay under a line of peppermint willow trees, the three men climbed out and went to stand by the waist-high weldmesh fence next to the main terminal. As they stood watching the lights of a small aircraft approaching from the east, their breath condensed in the chill desert air.

'Temp sure drops at night out here in the sticks,' Craig muttered, rubbing both arms and then wincing when his hands found some tender bruising.

Bugs dug him in the ribs. 'You gettin' soft old son? Too much pencil-pushin'?' This earned him a disgruntled, 'Humph.'

At a sudden squawk of tyres on tarmac, they turned to see the light plane touch down on the main runway. It taxied toward the terminal at first, and then veered toward the three men as if having spotted them. They stood silently watching as the plane slowed and came to a stop in front of them, then the rear hatch and stairs were lowered as its twin engines whirred to a stop.

Seeing Ben's hulking frame squeeze through the opening, Bugs and Craig collected their duffels and all three jumped the fence to meet Ben halfway.

Dropping a spare duffel at Spooky's feet, Ben barked, 'You can suit up when we're in the air. We're leaving in five.'

'In *that* thing?' Frowning, Bugs tilted his head toward the King Air. 'The Huey'll cut it to shreds.'

In answer Ben looked to the east, to where twin lights approached fast and low over the terrain.

When Craig ventured, 'Is that a Taipan?' Ben checked the tracking app on his phone and turned narrowed, thoughtful eyes on Bugs. 'You've given me an idea.'

'Oh?'

'Yeah. The Huey has passed between Mount Isa and Cloncurry, still heading north. We'll need the fastest transport on hand to catch it.'

'So … the Taipan?' The hopeful light in Bugs' eyes dimmed when Ben shook his head and made for the King Air.

The pilot was walking around the aircraft carrying out a visual inspection when Ben strode up to him. 'Don,' he said crisply, 'you got enough fuel to get us to Mount Isa?'

Turning to him with a question in his eyes, the pilot checked an app on his phone and gave a grudging nod. 'Yeah … but my orders were just to get you here.'

'Your orders are to do as I say,' Ben barked. 'Can you make arrangements to refuel at Mount Isa as soon as we land?'

'Yeah … but….' Don ran an agitated hand over his head and then sighed. 'You'd better have clearance for all this.'

'I'll worry about the clearance, you just make it happen.' Turning on his heels, Ben strode back to the others.

'We'd better be getting double time for this,' the co-pilot muttered dourly when Don squeezed into the seat beside his. Leaning forward to flick a switch on the instrument panel he groused, 'It's gonna be a long night.'

As soon as the Taipan touched down and its rotors slowed, Ben went to the cargo hold, slid open the door and climbed inside. After ducking his head into the cockpit to give the pilot instructions, he collected parachutes and handed them out to the other three men, along with MP5SD6 assault rifles and rounds of subsonic ammo. Grabbing the remaining chute, he jumped out and led the men back to the King Air.

At the roar of the Taipan's Rolls Royce engines Bugs glanced over his shoulder and then jogged up beside Ben. 'You serious? We're not goin' in the Taipan?'

Ben maintained his long-legged stride. 'We're short on time and the King Air is almost twice as fast as that chopper.'

Looking behind again, Bugs watched it take off. Banking left, the chopper headed back in the direction it had come.

As the four men climbed aboard the King Air, pilot Don frowned at Ben. 'What're the chutes for?' His frown deepened. 'Tell me you're not thinking of jumping out of this plane.' At Ben's quelling glance, he blustered, 'Now hang on! Chauffeuring you is one thing, but this aircraft isn't designed to be parachuted from.'

'Look,' Ben said with a long-suffering sigh, 'if we do need to jump, all you have to do is level off at eighteen thousand feet, depressurise the cab, extend the flaps, and slow her to eighty-five knots.'

Throwing him a dark look Don said tightly, 'I know how to fly the plane.'

'Good.' Ben settled himself into a seat. 'Then let's get going.'

• • •

'Hurry up and wait,' Wolf said broodingly, 'definitely feels like we're back in the Army again, 'specially with these blokes for company.' He indicated the two Army pilots of the C-27J Spartan seated nearby.

'So,' the senior pilot piped up, 'we've been here an hour. Any update on where we're going and what we're collecting?'

'Still waiting to hear our destination,' Modeen replied. 'And as far as I know, we're not collecting anything. It's just the two of us.'

The pilot frowned at her in disbelief. 'You mean a medium-sized transport, capable of carrying forty-six paratroopers or a payload of eleven and a half thousand kilos, was deployed to taxi you two around?'

Modeen gave a blithe nod, while Wolf shrugged and leaned back in his chair, putting his arms behind his head.

The pilot wasn't prepared to leave it there. 'You guys must be pretty special.'

'Well, we think so,' Modeen replied with a grin, and then lifted her chin at Wolf. 'Let's go check on Susan. Be good to get some fresh air and stretch our legs.'

He was on his feet before she finished speaking. They stepped out into the night and headed to the main administration building, where they stopped at the door to the first security cell. Solid hardwood, it sported a hefty double deadbolt lock and reinforced hinges. On Ben's orders the base had posted an armed guard at the door. He nodded at Wolf and Modeen and moved aside so they could look through the peep hole.

The cell's interior was more confortable than a prison but a long way from plush. It contained a single bunk, bedside table, and a writing desk. Susan Morris was stretched out on the bunk and appeared to be asleep.

When Modeen told him what she'd seen, Wolf asked, 'When will they move her?'

'Ben didn't say.' Modeen gazed at him thoughtfully. 'Guess he's got more important things on his mind at the moment.'

Forty kilometres due north of Mornington Island, the German-built, one-hundred and thirty-six metre-long Russian factory trawler *Oleg Moreplavatel* sat anchored by its six metre draught on the calm waters of the Gulf of Carpentaria. At super-trawler class, she was fitted with three huge gantries at the bow, stern, and mid-ships. The few areas of her nineteen metre-wide deck not covered in tons of old fishing nets, cable reels and other rigging equipment, were pitted and stained with rust and dried fish guts, evidence of her many years of service.

Her captain stood in front of the bridge tower windows, staring through a pair of high-powered Baigish binoculars. As the bright light in the sky over the island grew larger on approach, he lowered the binoculars and barked an order. A moment later flood lights illuminated a flat, clear section at the ship's bow.

The thump, thump, thump of the Huey grew to a thunderous pounding as it closed in on the trawler and streaked down her port side. Climbing, the chopper banked left and arced around to come to a hover above the ship's bow. A crew member in gumboots and shabby, stained overalls, took a wide stance on the platform as he was buffeted by the Huey's downdraft. Using a pair of orange marshalling wands, he guided the chopper down until the crate containing the stolen cargo settled gently on the deck. Then, after signalling the pilot to release the harness, he backed away as ten burly crew members moved in to remove the cargo.

Once the landing platform was clear, the Huey settled onto the deck and the whir of its rotors slowed as its cargo bay door slid open and eleven men climbed out. A tall, blonde Russian with a boxer's nose led his comrades across the deck to where the crate now sat. They gathered around it as the precious item was hitched to a block and tackle suspended from the twelve metre-high forward gantry. The crate rose slowly above the deck before being lowered into the ship's cargo hold.

With a curt nod, the man with the boxer's nose turned and barked orders, and watched as his men dispersed to take up strategic sentry points around the ship.

. . .

Ben swivelled to stretch his long legs into the aisle. Although the seats on the King Air were comfortable, the rows were too close together to give sufficient legroom for such a tall man. Thankfully they were on approach to Mount Isa for a refuelling stop.

Seeing him check the tracking app on his phone, Spooky leaned into the aisle and enquired, 'Where is it now?'

Ben zoomed in on TD5685 and said slowly, 'It has crossed the coastline … and come to a stop.'

'Whereabouts?'

'Out at sea.' Ben rubbed his chin. 'On the other side of Mornington Island.'

Spooky gazed levelly at him. 'Must be a ship out there big enough to land a chopper on.'

Checking the AIS Global Marine traffic app on his phone, Ben zoomed in on the Gulf of Carpentaria and shook his head. 'Well, if there is a ship out there it must have its transponder turned off.'

'Unless it's a military vessel, or maybe a submarine?'

'Yeah … but I reckon it's unlikely to be a sub.' Ben's eyes narrowed. 'However, you've given me an idea.' After scrolling through the contact list on his phone he bent his head, pressed the mobile against one ear, and cupped a hand over the other one to drown out the hum from the engines. He was soon engaged in more than one brisk, business-like conversation.

When he finished the final call and sat back in his

seat, Spooky looked over at him. 'You got back-up organised for us?'

Ben threw him a wry glance. *'We're* the back-up, Spook.'

'Who for? Clearance divers? Commandos?'

Ben's face split in a grin. 'Something even more deadly.'

'Yeah? What?'

'Wolf and Modeen.'

After boarding the waiting Spartan, Modeen and Wolf began strapping on their cumbersome HALO gear while in the cockpit the pilots, glad to finally have something to do, set the Dowdy six blade propellers of the twin engines in motion. As the transport prepared for take-off, Modeen and Wolf plugged the intercom cables into the audio jacks on their combat helmets, so they could communicate with the pilots up front.

'What's our ETA in Burketown?' Modeen's voice crackled into the pilot's ears.

There was a buzz of static before the senior pilot replied, 'An hour and two minutes from now.'

Wolf raised an eyebrow and joked, 'Can't this bucket go any faster?'

There was another buzz of static and then the pilot announced stiffly, 'Flight distance to Burketown is six hundred and twenty-five clicks, and our max cruising speed is six hundred KPH. Shouldn't be too hard for a couple of grunts like you to do the maths.'

Modeen grinned and rolled her eyes at Wolf. 'Seems these fly boys don't know how to take a joke.'

'It's OK.' He threw her a wink. 'We'll kill them last.'

'Very funny,' came the laconic reply from the cockpit.

When the King Air taxied to a stop after touching down at Mount Isa airport, Ben got out to stretch his legs. The sky above him was dark and the light breeze blowing across the apron held the desert-like chill of inland Australia. Seeing the fuel truck rumbling toward them over the floodlit tarmac, he took out his phone and checked the tracking app again. It appeared the Huey and its stolen cargo were still stationary out at sea, about fifteen minutes flying time, he calculated, from remote Burketown.

His expression thoughtful, he closed down the tracker and placed a call to Scherger base.

To flush the nitrogen from their bloodstream in preparation for the jump, Modeen and Wolf had been on pre-breathers for the last twenty-five minutes. Having made the final adjustments to their HALO chutes, they rifled through the night ops kits, taking out what they thought they'd need. After clipping MP5SD6 assault rifles to the front of their webbing, they moved to the back ramp, only to feel the aircraft bank and change course. They shared a glance as the senior pilot's voice crackled across the Spartan's intercom.

'Target has changed,' he said abruptly, 'we just got new coordinates. ETA fifteen minutes.'

There was a grin in the co-pilot's voice when he chimed in. 'I hope you brought wetsuits.'

Wolf frowned at Modeen. 'Wetsuits?'

'Yeah,' the co-pilot replied smugly, 'looks like you're going swimming.'

Wolf rolled his eyes. 'Where's the drop zone?'

'At sea.' The senior pilot came on again. 'About thirty clicks north of Mornington Island.'

Murmuring, 'Gotta be a boat or a ship,' Modeen felt the phone in the leg pocket of her cargos vibrate with an incoming text. Taking it out she saw *Target: Latitude: -15.714273 Longitude: 139.563904* on the screen.

Wolf moved closer. 'From Ben?'

She nodded. 'Coordinates.' When she tapped on the link in the text message, the phone's map app zoomed in on a point out to sea in the Gulf of Carpentaria. While holding out the mobile so Wolf could see the map, she checked the altimeter strapped to her forearm. Its two inch dial displayed an altitude of eighteen thousand feet.

She looked at Wolf. 'The higher we go, the harder it'll be for them to detect us.' At his thumbs-up signal, she announced over the comms, 'Take us up to thirty-five thousand feet.'

'Roger that, thirty-five angels,' came back from the cockpit. 'You've got seven minutes to drop zone.'

Sharing a nod of acknowledgement, Modeen and Wolf double and then triple-checked each other's AAD, oxygen bottles and connections. Taking the GPS from the night ops kit, Modeen entered the new coordinates before strapping it to her other wrist. Then she donned a pair of thermal gloves and dipped her head at Wolf. He stood, kitted and ready, beside the rear control panel on the side bulkhead. At her nod he thumbed up the centre red toggle guard and flicked the switch to the ON position.

As though the Spartan were a giant bird coming out of hibernation, its cargo hold took on a new life. The red hue of a warning strobe light bounced off its interior walls and a strident alarm resonated throughout, as the rear ramp slowly cranked open. Its larger, top section opened upward and inward, while the shorter bottom section moved lower and outward until horizontal.

The rush of chill night air tugged at Modeen and Wolf as the ramp locked into position. They stood with their legs apart for stability, gripping the cable running along the side wall with one hand while staring out into the darkness. It was o-three thirty and heavy clouds blocked the pale light from a crescent moon.

The co-pilot's voice crackled over the comms. 'Two minutes to drop zone.'

At his words, Modeen and Wolf switched from the pre-breathers to their oxygen bottles. Then, pulling curved thirty round magazines from their webbing, they locked and loaded their assault rifles.

'Thirty seconds to drop zone. Go on green,' the co-pilot announced. 'And good luck, grunts. Happy hunting.'

Wolf gave an amused snort and growled, 'Alpha Mike Foxtrot,' before unplugging the comms jack from his helmet and flicking the cable to the side. He took up position at the start of the ramp, and when the red warning light turned to green and the alarm changed to a solid beep, he gestured for Modeen to take the lead.

Following a quick check of the GPS on her wrist, she jogged to the end of the ramp and dived into the darkness, arms outstretched. After giving her a second's head start, he followed her out.

In the cockpit the co-pilot toggled the controls to close the ramp. With a wry grin at the pilot beside him he said, 'Reckon he meant that in a friendly way?'

The pilot cocked an eyebrow at him and shrugged.

'ALARM, ALARM!' The warning shout came from the sentry stationed high above the deck on the centre gantry of the *Oleg Moreplavatel*. He cupped his ears and squinted into the sky, trying to locate the source of the faint drone coming from high overhead. He was quickly joined by two of his comrades.

As the sound faded into the distance, one of them said in guttural Russian, 'It is nothing.'

'I tell you,' the first sentry argued, 'I heard an aircraft fly over us.'

The others were already heading back to their stations. One of them muttered over his shoulder, 'A passenger plane, perhaps, headed for New Guinea or the Philippines.'

On the landing outside the bridge at the top of the ship's four-storey bridge tower, the man with the boxer's nose gave a dismissive grunt and stepped back inside. Slapping the captain on a shoulder, he said triumphantly, 'We are all going to be very rich, comrade. And once we have delivered our cargo, mother Russia will again be a world super power.' His eyes narrowed. 'One to be reckoned with.'

CHAPTER EIGHTEEN

As she plummeted at terminal velocity through the cold, high altitude air, Modeen's GPS guided her toward a faint light in the dark expanse of the Gulf. She adjusted course to head for the target as the dial of the altimeter on her forearm rapidly wound down counter-clockwise.

In the sky above and slightly to the left of her, Wolf noticed the gap between them closing. He de-arched, knowing if he didn't take measures to slow his descent, his heavier build would see him overtake her.

As they bore down onto the dark mass of the factory trawler, it began to take shape against the equally dark water. After almost two minutes of free-fall they were at six thousand feet. When Modeen bent one arm back and pointed her thumb at her chute pack with exaggerated up and down movements, Wolf banked further left to give her more room. He saw her reach around for her drogue, and released his chute at the same time. As the wing-shaped, ram-air canopies of their elliptical chutes filled with air and pulled them up at five thousand feet, they snapped down the night vision goggles mounted on top of their helmets.

Utilising her high performance canopy's greater manoeuvrability thanks to its radical tapered shape, Modeen swung left, giving two straight arm signals to indicate she would take the stern while Wolf was to land mid-ships. As she continued quietly downward through the night air, she glimpsed a sentry positioned at the top of the rear gantry. Taking her silenced Walter PPQ from the inside of her vest, she swooped past and neutralised the sentry with a quick double tap. Then, banking sharply right, she circled and dropped to the deck at the rear of the ship, landing in the centre of the trawl loading ramp.

In the air above, Wolf unclipped his assault rifle. As he came in over the twin exhaust funnels rear of mid-ships, the sentry on the middle gantry had his back to him. Swooping down and then banking hard one-eighty degrees, heading for a clear patch on top of the ship's bridge tower, Wolf came dangerously close to the communications mast that rose from a cross beam on the roof above the bridge.

The guard standing on the platform to the left of the mast gave a start and raised his AK47. Wolf let loose a short burst from his MP5 and the subsonic bullets made muffled thuds as they hit the guard's chest. The man slumped onto the railing just as a gust of wind caught Wolf's chute. It threw him to the right and into the communications tower, entangling the cords in the rotating arm of the radar antenna. Swung around hard like a helpless string-puppet, he was sent crashing against one of the steel pylons supporting the tower.

Swinging to a stop and dangling between the pylons two metres above the roof of the bridge, Wolf blinked and shook his head in frustration. While his position provided no cover, it gave him a bird's eye view of the ship's expansive rear deck. When he heard a burst from an AK47, his head snapped up.

As bullets ricocheted off the ramp close by her, Modeen dived to the side, hastily shrugging out of her chute. Ripping the oxygen mask from her face, she tossed it to the side and crouched on the deck, peering upward, trying to make her assailant's position. She saw a man jerk and then sag against the middle gantry's railing. His body dropped to the floor, then slid under the mid-rail to tumble, limp and lifeless, to the deck twelve metres below.

Lights blazed on as alarms rang out around the ship. The powerful beams of searchlights mounted at the front and rear of the bridge tower began scouring the deck, moving side to side and occasionally up and down, probing the darkness.

Realising he was dangerously exposed, Wolf used another short burst from his MP5 to sever the chute cords holding him in place. They snapped, dropping him onto the roof of the bridge tower. He tried to land upright but his feet slipped out from under him and he fell heavily on his back, letting out a grunt as the air was punched from his lungs. While the reserve chute in his backpack provided some cushioning against the solid metal roof, it was his helmet he was most thankful for. It saved him from suffering a mild concussion.

At the rear of the main deck, Modeen sprinted up the ramp and took cover in an overhang at the base of the rear gantry. From there she climbed the metal ladder fitted to its left side, and came to a stop behind a cable reel on a platform fixed to the gantry three metres above the deck. She waited for the rear searchlight to sweep past and then took it out with a burst from her silenced MP5. The light exploded with a loud pop and a shower of glass.

Seconds later, the deck to her right was peppered with a volley of heavy gunfire. Taking cover behind the gantry's rusted pillar, she peered up to where the shots had come from and saw a man on the bridge tower. He was working the controls of a high-calibre, tripod-mounted Kord-6P50 machine gun.

Switching her MP5 to single shot, she clicked up her night vision goggles and took aim through the rifle's thermal scope. She watched the man spray another volley across the deck in the hope of flushing out a target. Steadying herself against the upright, Modeen squeezed her rifle's trigger and an instant later the man staggered back from the machine gun, clutching his throat. He fell against the wall of the bridge behind him and slid down it sideways, leaving a wet crimson trail in his wake.

While the man lay gurgling and writhing in his death throes, on the roof above Wolf shrugged off his chute's harness. Rolling onto his stomach with a stifled groan, he got to his feet while taking care to stay low, and moved to the front of the bridge tower. In the side-to-side sweeps of the forward searchlight, he glimpsed a Huey at the bow of the ship. The chopper's khaki paint job was chipped and faded, many of its panels badly dented. Probably ex-Army surplus, he decided.

Looking down, he saw a man on a narrow ledge about two metres directly below him standing behind a tripod-mounted M60 machine gun. To his left, another man operated the forward searchlight. Clicking his MP5 to single shot, Wolf eased it silently over the edge and fired off two rounds. He then switched it back to auto and strafed the rear of the searchlight's metal casing, where the wiring loom entered a junction box. He saw sparks and a small flame erupt as the wires shorted out, and then the light's beam flickered, grew dull, and finally extinguished.

• • •

Fifteen minutes south of Burketown the Beechcraft King Air cruised at twenty-five thousand feet, closing fast on its destination. A clearly restless Bugs paced up and down the aisle, stretching his legs and rolling his broad shoulders, until Ben rose from his seat and indicated with a lift of his chin for the others to follow suit. The four men filled the aisle's narrow space with their brawny bulk.

Making eye contact with each of them, Ben ordered, 'Time to suit up.' As they grabbed their gear he raised his voice to be heard above the aircraft's twin engines. 'I can't provide more specific details, but I can tell you we'll be deploying at eighteen thousand feet, onto what I believe is a vessel anchored in the Gulf. They won't be expecting an incursion from a light aircraft like this, so we should have the element of surprise on our side. All the same, follow me down and don't deploy your chutes until the last minute.' He eyeballed Spooky. 'Can you provide a description of the unit we're to recover, and what we might be up against?' It was an order more than a question.

'The electronic device we're looking for is a prototype fitted to the lightweight section of an airframe,' Spooky announced. 'It's housed in a khaki-coloured, metal module, rectangular in shape, one and a half metres wide by two metres long, by one and a half metres deep. It has two glass domes at opposing ends and electrical couplings down one side.'

Ben's eyes narrowed. 'And what sort of resistance are we likely to encounter?'

'There are at least eleven insurgents,' Spooky went on. 'Nine confirmed by you,' and he indicated Bugs and Craig, 'and two by me. I would expect at least double that number again on the vessel, probably all well armed.'

'I've received confirmation that Modeen and Wolf have deployed,' Ben cut in, 'so hopefully they'll provide cover for our approach.'

Bugs frowned at him. 'Modeen and Wolf? I thought they'd … you know … left the organisation. So how'd you get 'em to sign up for this?'

'Long story,' Ben said crisply. 'Let's just say they were in the wrong place at the right time, and felt compelled to lend a hand.' After pausing to check his phone, he raised his voice again. 'We've got about twelve minutes to the jump zone, so check your gear and ready yourselves.'

Squeezing past Bugs, he pulled Craig aside and said quietly, 'You comfortable with the jump? I know you don't have a military background.'

Craig gave a confident nod. 'Not a problem. I completed over fifty solo jumps after doing my NatSec training.'

'Good.' Ben thumped him on a shoulder and then turned to address the group again. 'I'll jump first, followed by Spook and Craig. Bugs, you'll be our tail-end Charlie. Need you to watch our backs when we hit the deck.'

The three men nodded their acknowledgement and proceeded to don their combat helmets and check their comms units, while Ben made his way to the cockpit to give the pilots their final instructions.

CHAPTER NINETEEN

With a harsh metallic clang, the small pineapple grenade bounced off one of the pylons and skidded to a stop a short distance away from Wolf. Leaping to his feet as his reflexes kicked in, he sprinted for the rear of the bridge tower roof and dived behind a pile of old rigging rope. As he flattened himself against the deck plate, the grenade exploded. Metal ricocheted off metal as potentially lethal fragments sprayed the area around him.

As the explosion's after-effects subsided, he heard a voice yelling orders from the bridge. Lifting his head, he saw men scurrying up the side of the bridge tower.

Time to move.

Using the rigging rope, he slipped silently off the roof and lowered himself down to the next level.

.   .   .

On the left side of the rear gantry, Modeen paused at the base of the metal ladder to check for any signs her position had been made.

There were none.

Having taken out the rear searchlight, along with the machine gunner, she was free to circle around under the winch platform. Coming across a small hatch cover, she bent to remove it and then listened for any activity.

All seemed dark and quiet. A faint stench of rotting seafood rose from below.

Grasping the top rung of the narrow metal ladder, she slipped into the access port and climbed down to the first level below deck. She glanced around, taking in the various conveyors running up, down, and across the cavernous space. Some of the belts were lined with thick black rubber, others interwoven stainless steel plates. All were flanked by rows of metal trays and off-ramps leading to what she guessed were gutting, fillet-ing, and guillotining machines.

The dimly lit room was obviously the super trawler's sorting and processing area. The equipment sat idle, and didn't appear to have been used for some time. The atmosphere inside the room was cloying and heavy with the stale reek of rotten fish, making Modeen screw up her nose and regret having ditched her oxygen mask.

Trying to keep her breathing shallow, she crept along a narrow walkway. It took her on a zigzag course between the conveyors and an assortment of different types of control stations, augers, electrical motors and switch panels.

Outside the rear wall of the bridge, Wolf peered through a porthole at three men huddled around a central map table. When a tall blonde man turned side-on, bringing his prominent boxer's nose into view, Wolf's eyes narrowed. And when he glimpsed the edge of a crepe bandage peeking out from the man's right cuff, his lips twisted in a triumphant grin.

'Erik,' The man barked into a hand-held two-way. When there was no reply he said more loudly, 'Erik!'

Static was the only sound that greeted him.

'Uri.'

Nothing.

'Uri, ANSWER!'

Still no response.

With a frustrated, 'Argh!' and flinging the radio onto the table, he turned to the man nearest him. Yelling, '*Idti. Idti!*' he pointed to the door.

Outside, Wolf backed away, looking for the best escape route. The nearby handrail was his only option. After climbing it he hung there briefly, waiting for an opportunity to drop to the deck below without having the sound announce his presence. When a group of men left the bridge, he used the noise of their heavy footsteps and guttural chatter to mask his movements. Once on the lower level, he kept his head down as he continued descending to the base of the bridge tower, one level above the main deck. He headed around the front of the tower toward the bow of the ship, hugging the shadows and keeping his footfalls as light as is possible for a big man.

When the shot rang out, Modeen jerked back.

Too late.

The bullet tore through the sleeve of her black jacket and ricocheted off the conveyors behind her. She felt a searing sensation just below her shoulder and clutched her arm. Ducking forward, she took cover behind an electrical cabinet and peered in the direction she figured the bullet had come from.

Movement between a grated metal stairwell and stainless steel vat caught her eye. Vying for a better angle, she crouched lower, scanning for further activity. The narrow walkway hindered her movements so she slung the assault rifle over her shoulder and took the Walther PPQ from inside her jacket.

Her view was restricted by all the metal brackets, uprights and machinery in the room. When she glimpsed a shadow moving further to her left, she dropped on her side and pressed her cheek to the floor to stare through the forest of metal legs and other supports.

In the dimness, a boot moved stealthily to join its stationary mate.

Blat, blat!

She heard a grunt of pain and saw the shadow drop to the floor with a thud. To make sure it wouldn't get up again, she fired another two rounds. The shadow gasped, twitched, and grew still.

Modeen was about to rise to her feet when *CRASH*, a metal bowl fell to the floor sounding more like a crash symbol on a drum kit. The clamour resonated throughout as the bowl rattled to a stop. Hearing a frustrated exhalation from ahead of her position, she folded herself into a compact space between the middle shelf and the conveyor … and waited.

As a second shadow approached from around the corner, its movements wary but determined, she clicked down her night vision goggles. They revealed a heavily-built man in camo cargo pants and dark T-shirt. From her position in the shelf just a foot off the floor, she couldn't see his face.

She aimed her pistol and watched him approach, his movements increasingly tentative as though he was aware of lurking danger. As he brought his right foot forward, the knee cap above it exploded, and his leg buckled under his weight. He let out a roar and fell, clutching his knee, as Modeen fired again.

A head shot this time.

Changing the clip in her PPQ, she unfolded herself and got to her feet to stare down at the dead man. His blonde hair was pulled back in a greasy man-bun, and something about his tall build looked familiar. Could he be the Russian who'd attacked them in Melbourne? She grabbed a fistful of bun and ripped his head sideways.

He had a long, straight nose.

Not the Russian … at least, not the one she was hoping for.

With a disappointed huff she let his head clunk to the floor, before turning to check his pockets.

Two spare eighteen round, nine millimetre clips.

Handy.

While the clips wouldn't fit her pistol, the ammo certainly would. After packing the bullets into a spare pocket on her cargos with swift efficiency, she rose and made her way out.

At the sound of approaching footsteps, Wolf ducked behind a winch reel guard and carefully slipped one of the titanium knives from its scabbard. He crouched, motionless, as the guard armed with an assault rifle marched past. A few moments later, Wolf was behind the man cupping a large hand over his mouth and dragging him back into the shadows. After lying the body where it wouldn't be easily seen, he continued on.

Spotting a small hatch near the port gunwale, he checked the area was clear and then made for it. When he opened the hatch, light radiated up at him from what appeared to be a brightly illuminated room below. The hatch only offered a limited field of vision, so he leaned in closer for a better look. He could see pallets, stacked to the ceiling with clear plastic-wrapped piles of flat-pack boxes. He eyed the solid metal workbench nearby, thinking it would provide good cover. After pushing the lid of the hatch fully open, he descended the narrow metal ladder, only stopping to pull the hatch cover closed behind him.

When he reached the workbench Wolf crouched behind it and surveyed his surroundings. On the other side of the room another long metal bench was connected to conveyors and rollers on both sides. A tall packing station used to automate the packing and binding of the boxes, dominated the bench's centre.

All was quiet.

Before breaking cover he unclipped the night vision goggles from the top of his helmet, fastening them to a small karabiner on his webbing. Making for a room off to the right, toward the front of the ship, he came to a heavy sliding door. It sat open. The room beyond it was warm, the fans of the wall-mounted evaporator units silent.

This must be the freezer storage section. Not in operation, like other parts of the ship.

He stuck his head around the door to peer into the room, but jerked back as a hail of bullets peppered the wall on the other side of his position. He gave a grunt.

Not in operation, but also not empty.

When a commotion broke out inside the room, he darted back to the metal bench and slid over it, as another volley of bullets clanked around him. Moving to the bench's forward edge he peered around it to see a Balkancar electric forklift emerge from the freezer room. A raised pallet of boxes effectively shielded the driver as he turned the yellow Balkancar sharply and charged toward Wolf, obviously intent on crushing him between the bench and the ship's hull.

Ducking as bullets ricocheted off the bench and around him, Wolf knew he had to move, and find a way to neutralise the driver.

Keeping low, he dived right and to the floor. Sliding on his back he fired off two rounds as he skidded to a stop next to a stack of boxes. He rolled and pressed his back against the stack, and watched as the forklift driver lurched back and then slumped forward onto the steering wheel. The forklift slowed but continued its forward progress until it came up against the bench with a loud screech of metal against metal. The heavy impact drove the bench backward a few inches.

Seeing the driver's flaccid body sag from the cab and fall to the floor, Wolf was about to break cover when another two men raced from the freezer room to storm his position. Wolf dropped them with a burst from his rifle, only to see several more of their comrades take cover behind the conveyor and packing station on the opposite side of the room.

He was pinned down.

Tightening his grip on the MP5, Wolf looked around hoping to find a way out … or better cover at least.

At the sound of muffled gunfire from somewhere forward of mid-ship, Modeen's head shot up and she whipped around.

Troy.

She headed for the sound. Climbing the stairs at the far end of the room, she put her shoulder against the solid hatch and shoved it open. Pausing there, she gazed down the narrow corridor.

Empty.

Quiet.

She stepped out and made her way down the corridor which took her right, toward the ship's starboard side, and then left.

At least it's heading in the right direction, and it doesn't stink like that damn processing room.

Coming to a corner, she stopped to peer around it. The sixteen metre section of corridor had eight doors lining its right side, and two along the left, both evenly spaced halfway down. Moving to the first door she put an ear close and listened for any sounds of movement.

Nothing.

She gave the handle a turn.

Still nothing.

Putting her foot against the door, she shoved it open.

Silence greeted her.

She stepped inside. The almost two metre square cabin contained a single bunk bed, tucked into a corner, and a porthole at the far end with a compact writing desk beneath it.

Crew quarters.

Her head shot up when another muffled exchange of gunfire rang out and she hurried from the cabin. Making her way past the doors on her right, she made for the first of the two on the left. Through its circular glass window she could see into the ship's galley and crew's mess. It looked unoccupied, so she pressed on to the end of the corridor. At the hatch she noticed a set of internal stairs running upward on the left.

She paused, considering where to go from there.

Above, in the bridge tower, the captain turned and shouted in Russian, 'Aircraft approaching from the south.'

Cursing loudly in his mother tongue, the man with the boxer's nose flung the contents of the central map table across the floor of the bridge. A dark flush infused his face as he snatched up a two-way handset and bellowed in Russian, 'Drop the forward derrick arm onto the roof of the bridge. And prepare the chopper for take-off.'

'That's our target, there.' Ben leaned between the pilot and co-pilot and pointed through the cockpit window at a faint light in the vast blackness of the Gulf. 'Keep to this heading and drop to eighteen thousand. Then throttle back and depressurise the cabin.'

'Well … OK.' The pilot gave a slow, dubious shake of his head. 'It's your call.' Clearly unhappy with what was about to transpire, he wasn't going to argue with a six foot four giant armed with an assault rifle and oozing authority from every pore.

Turning, Ben squeezed past Spooky, Bugs and Craig standing prepped and ready in the aisle, and positioned himself near the rear exit hatch. He heard the engine note change and felt the plane slow and lose altitude, and glanced at his GPS. When he looked up again he saw the pilot craning his neck to gaze into the passengers' compartment. At the pilot's thumbs-up signal, Ben dipped his head in acknowledgement and turned to the hatch, as the other three men made their way down the aisle to join him.

Pressing the release button, he cranked the handle counter-clockwise. A warning alarm sounded in the cabin as he pushed the top of the door outward. As it dropped slowly, brisk morning air rushed in, buffeting the four men. They grabbed onto nearby seats to steady themselves as the drag created by the heavy hatch's thick profile caused the plane's tail to slew sharply. Up front, the pilot stomped on the left rudder pedal to adjust the aircraft's yaw. Once the plane was steady and back on course, he threw his co-pilot an exasperated glance. In the main cabin, their four passengers bunched up and, without any ceremony, exited the plane in single file to disappear into the darkness.

'They're out.' At the pilot's shout, the co-pilot unclipped his seatbelt and hurried to the back of the plane. The pilot called after him, 'Watch yourself with that open hatch.'

Taking a lanyard from the rear compartment, the co-pilot wrapped one end around his waist and secured the other end to the base of the nearest seat. Careful to brace himself with one hand, he grabbed the aft cable with the other and pulled. The door, with its inlay of deep steps, moved reluctantly, the wind-drag making it extra heavy. His muscles strained and he braced a foot on the fuselage for extra leverage. Bunching up and grasping the cable with both hands, he managed to bring the door three quarters of the way up.

Seeing his co-pilot struggling to close the hatch, the pilot rolled the plane to the right and the door's weight shifted over centre. At another tug from the co-pilot the hatch slammed closed, the force making him stumble back. Gripping the cable firmly, he dragged himself forward to crank the handle clockwise. The warning alarm cut out and silence settled on the cabin again as he sagged back against the bulkhead. He waited to catch his breath before making his way back to the cockpit.

The pilot watched him take his seat again and threw him a grateful nod. 'Well done. Now let's get the hell outta here.'

Slipping through the hatch, Modeen breathed in a lungful of fresh sea air while getting her bearings. Behind her the bridge tower loomed five storeys above, while directly ahead and downward she saw an old Huey sitting on the ship's bow. At the sound of a light plane overhead she peered upward, straining to locate the aircraft – or parachutes – in the dark sky. To get a better view she ducked back inside and ran lightly up the stairs leading to the bridge.

At the front of the bridge tower one of the sentries callously shoved aside his comrade's corpse with a boot. Taking up position behind the tripod-mounted M60 machine gun, he also strained his eyes and ears upward as the drone of a light aircraft faded into the distance. Hidden in the darkness above him, four black ram-air canopies opened in quick succession and filled with air, as Ben and his team spiralled downward toward the trawler.

On the ship below them, Modeen came to the top of the steps and then hurried down a corridor and up another single flight of stairs, before exiting through a hatch onto the deck alongside the bridge. Pressing herself against the wall, she saw a sentry at the front corner rail point his AK47 into the sky above the bow of the ship. She set off at a run, firing her pistol and hitting him in the shoulder. He gave a cry and jerked violently backward, clutching at his shoulder, as she continued toward him.

When the deep rat-a-tat-tat of the M60 started up to his right, she quickened her pace. The injured man spun around as she fired again, and his head snapped backward. Springing in the air, she kicked off him and launched herself sideways while sending his limp body over the metre-high railing. Still in mid-air, she spun one-eighty degrees and took out the M60 gunner with a single shot, before landing on her side on the deck. Satisfied she had neutralised the immediate threat, she sat up to watch as four dark figures glided downward. When movement inside the bridge caught her attention, she leapt to her feet. Sprinting back to the heavy side hatch, she wrenched it open and peered cautiously inside.

In the darkness behind her, the four shadowy figures landed soundlessly on the deck at the base of the bridge tower. After dumping their chutes they took cover, until a muffled burst of heavy gunfire coming from the forward deck below their position had them vaulting over the railing. Dropping two metres to the level below, they zeroed in on the gunfire and searched for an entry hatch. Spooky's keen eyes located one near the portside gunwale and he signalled them over.

As the four men were disappearing below deck, above them Modeen was crouching low and entering the bridge, checking to right and left as she went. She saw a figure, the captain by the look of the stained woollen watch cap on his head, sitting at the map table with his back to her.

'Hands up!' When the man didn't move she tried Russian. '*Ruki vverkh!*'

Still no reaction.

Approaching warily, she poked him in the shoulder with the silencer of her pistol and immediately stepped back, ready for a violent reaction. Instead of whipping around to confront her, he slumped in the chair as his head sagged onto his chest. She frowned and swivelled the chair to face her, the movement causing his limp body to slip to one side. A bead of dark blood at the end of the ooze line from the hole in his forehead, dripped greasily onto his pants.

At the screech of a rusty pulley just outside the bridge, Modeen whipped her head up and glimpsed a dark shape sailing downward past the front window. She raced forward to see the figure of a tall man on a flying fox gliding beneath a derrick arm to the bow of the ship. A metre above the deck he released his hold and dropped at the derrick's base, to sprint toward the Huey. When he passed beneath a light she caught the glint of blonde hair.

Rushing outside through the heavy hatch, Modeen circled around to the front of the bridge, unslinging her MP5 as she ran. Climbing up the guard rail, she balanced on the top and slipped the rifle over the cable below the arm. With one hand on the stock and the other grasping the rifle's barrel, she kicked herself off the edge and sailed downward.

On the bow, the chopper's blades spun into motion and the Huey began rising from the deck. Not waiting to finish the ride, Modeen released her grip on the rifle and dropped the last two metres, landing at the base of the gantry support. Seeing the Huey turn and power across the front of the ship, she made for it, sprinting at full pace and then launching herself into mid-air, arms outstretched. Her right hand connected with the nearest of the chopper's landing skids and she clamped down hard.

The deep thump, thump of the Huey's motor pounded through her bones, and turbulence from its blades threatened to dislodge her, as she threw her other hand upward and pulled herself on board.

Below deck Wolf's ammo was all but out. After firing the last round from his Glock, he tossed it to the side and pulled one of the blue knives from its scabbard. He crouched, ready to drive the blade into the first attacker to come at him over the bench, when a hail of bullets erupted from deep within the freezer room. He froze and then raised his head to risk a look at his attackers. They were now aiming in the direction the shots had come from, but before they could fire their weapons, the conveyer they were using as cover was peppered with bullets.

A chorus of expletives and pained bellows followed, accompanied by the thuds of multiple bodies hitting the floor and the clatter of dropped weapons. A moment later Wolf saw the large bulk of a familiar figure exiting the freezer room, leading with an MP5. As he got to his feet, Wolf's lips tipped into a relieved grin as another smaller, but just as familiar, figure followed the first one out.

Calling, 'It's me, guys,' he broke cover, stepping into the middle of the room. The two men lowered their weapons and came closer to bump his outstretched fist. He grinned and shook his head. 'Boy, am I glad to see you blokes. I was down to throwin' knives and harsh language.' When Bugs and Craig joined them, he frowned at the door and then at Ben. 'Where's Jo?'

'We saw her up on the bridge tower, just before we dropped in.'

'Yeah,' Spooky said, 'and it was lucky for us she was there to take out the machine gunner who'd been giving us some stick.'

With a crisp, 'Take Bugs and Craig and go find her,' to Wolf, Ben turned back to the freezer room. 'Spook and I are gonna check out the module.'

As the Huey levelled to hover above the trawler a hundred metres off its starboard side, its pilot pulled a small black box about the size of a cigarette pack from a pocket in his pants. Fitted with a single toggle switch and guard, green and red LEDs and a push button, the transmitter looked crudely made. It was obviously functional, however, for the man lifted the toggle guard and fixed the switch to the ON position. With a disdainful sniff of his misshapen nose, the man smirked down at the trawler as the green LED blinked on.

Through twisted lips he sneered in Russian, 'If my country can't have this prototype, then no one—' His eyes widened in shock as he felt cold steel press against his neck. An instant later his head jerked forward as a nine millimetre bullet pierced the base of his skull.

Standing behind him, Modeen caught the transmitter in her free hand when his grip faltered as his body went limp. She stared at the box for a split second and then flicked down the toggle guard. When the green LED went out, she slipped the transmitter into a pocket, and then hurried to drag the big man's body from the pilot's seat.

When one of his legs hooked around the cyclic stick, the chopper's nose lifted into a climb. Hastily dumping the body in the cargo bay, Modeen centred the stick as she settled herself into the now vacant pilot's seat. She had been at the stick of a Huey as part of her SAS training and was familiar with the operation of the throttle, collective, and rudder controls. Recalling her instructor's emphasis on the need for firm, smooth movements, she pushed the cyclic stick forward and to the right, bringing the chopper around.

She made for the bow of the ship again, thankful for the calm water as she managed to land the Huey with a crunch and scrape of skids. Glad to be safely down, she shut off the engine as Wolf, Bugs and Craig came running across the deck toward the helipad.

Climbing out of the cargo hold, she jogged to where the three men now stood at the edge of the pad, and was immediately pulled into a hug.

Frowning at her torn and bloodied sleeve, Wolf held her out and said gruffly, 'You OK?'

'Yeah, it's just a nick.' Turning, she fist-bumped Bugs and then held her fist out to Craig.

He merely gaped at her, appearing taken aback.

'C'mon mate.' Bugs gave a bark of laughter and dug him in the ribs. 'Don't leave 'er hangin'.'

'Sorry.' A chagrined Craig bumped her fist. 'Just … when they said Jo, I wasn't expecting … you know … um … you.'

Wolf raised a dark eyebrow at him and slipped a possessive arm around Modeen's waist. 'C'mon, Ben and Spook are down below checkin' out the module.'

She turned to him with a frown. 'Do they know about the bomb?'

He froze. 'What bomb?'

'Blondie was about to blow something to hell.' Pulling the transmitter from her pocket, she tossed it to Bugs.

He stared at it and then pressed a finger to the comms unit in his ear. 'Ahh … guys? The ship might be rigged to blow, so don't touch nothin'.'

Having just removed the inspection cowling from the laser module, Ben and Spooky were about to lay it on the ground when Bugs' announcement came over the comms.

They locked eyes and stiffened.

Finally Ben broke the silence. 'Easy. Lower it gently.' Once it was down and stable, he sat back and breathed out before barking into the comms, 'Any idea where, and what type of bomb we're looking for?'

Bugs glanced at Modeen. At her shrug he said, 'That's a negative, Ben.' He looked at the transmitter in his hand. 'All we know is it was gonna be detonated by remote transmitter,' adding, 'We're on our way down to you now.'

In the freezer room, they found Spooky stretched out on the floor with a compact torch in his hand. He was shining it beneath the hardwood pallet supporting the laser module.

At his triumphant, 'Found it!' Ben got down next to him and peered to where the torch beam illuminated three banks of C4 explosives. They were strapped together with a transceiver and detonator attached.

Keeping the torch focused on the device, Spooky murmured, 'Looks fairly basic. Do you want me to disarm it?'

Ben frowned. 'No,' and then sat up. 'Modeen and Wolf, I want you to stay here and keep the module secure. The rest of us will do a sweep of the ship and pick up any stragglers. The HMAS *Wollongong* should be coming around the tip of the cape any minute. We'll let her clearance divers deal with this.'

———

Dawn broke as the *Wollongong* anchored in the calm waters of the gulf alongside the *Oleg Moreplavatel*, the super trawler dwarfing the fifty-seven metre long Armidale-class patrol boat. From where they stood guard over a group of fourteen shabbily-dressed men, none of who admitted to speaking English and all of who looked to be either grease monkeys or kitchen staff, Bugs, Spooky and Craig greeted the clearance divers as they came on board. Ben met the patrol boat captain for a quick debrief and handover, before returning below deck to join Wolf and Modeen at the module.

'Thanks for keeping watch JD, Wolf,' Ben said. 'I've just briefed Jack on the situation. He's sending a Chinook to collect the module, and asked me to pass on his personal thanks to both of you for your assistance.' Ben gave a lopsided grin. 'He also wants to know if you'd consider coming back to NatSec.'

Modeen arched an eyebrow at him. 'I thought I was persona non grata after … you know.'

'Yeah.' Ben gave an amused grunt. 'But apparently you've redeemed yourself in Jack's eyes. He copped a lot of flack from the Pentagon but they're happy now the prototype – and Morris – are safe.'

'So, what happens now?'

'Well, Morris and his wife are on their way to Melbourne to be reunited, and the Yanks are talking about taking them both back to the States. They're keen to finalise the project, and don't want Morris or the laser out of their sight from here on in.'

At the sound of approaching footsteps, Ben turned

to see two clearance divers enter the room. 'Need you all to vacate,' one of them said politely. He strode up to Ben. 'We're evacuating the ship, sir, before we disarm the device.'

At his words Wolf ushered Modeen toward the door and drawled, 'Don't need to tell us twice.'

CHAPTER TWENTY-ONE

*S*ix *months later…*

Vases of white and pink-champagne roses filled the back room of the Return Services League clubhouse in Sydney's Darling Harbour, their perfume filling the intimate, sunlit space. Soft instrumental music greeted John and Freda Modeen as they entered the small but tastefully decorated room. Narrowing his eyes, he glanced around and gave a contemptuous sniff.

'Come now, John,' Freda said quietly, careful to keep the smile on her face, 'this is their day, Josephine's and Troy's. Don't do anything to spoil it.'

'But why did they decide to have it *here?*' He swept a dismissive hand around the room. 'Hardly a venue fitting for the wedding of a magistrate's daughter.'

Freda stopped to fix him with a level gaze. 'Perhaps, but with both of them being ex-soldiers, the RSL is probably the most appropriate venue.'

John carried on as though she hadn't spoken. 'They could've had the Gentlemen's Club, I had it all arranged.'

'But love, they told us right from the start they wanted to keep it low-key.'

John frowned. 'It could've been low key at the Club. I didn't reserve the ballroom for them, only one of the smaller function rooms.'

Freda gave a low laugh. 'Even so, with its white-gloved wait staff, crystal chandeliers and silver cande-labras, they wouldn't feel comfortable letting their hair down at your club.' She grinned up at him. 'Let's face it, you wouldn't be able to resist making it the wedding of the year, and your daughter knows that.' At the stubborn set of his lips, she tugged on his arm. 'This is how she wants it, John. We should be glad she agreed to a traditional wedding, and didn't want to get married while jumping out of a plane, or something.'

He raised an eyebrow at her as she continued.

'And you said you were pleased she's keeping her maiden name.' When he nodded, she gave him a gentle nudge. 'So c'mon, let's just enjoy celebrating the marriage of our only child.' Eyeing an unusually well-groomed Wolf greeting guests at the door and looking dapper but uneasy in a cobalt-grey, three-piece suit, she said dreamily, 'And even *you'd* have to admit the groom scrubs up well.'

At his disdainful grunt, she swatted John on the arm with a manicured hand. 'Well *I* think he fits the bill nicely. We always knew our girl wouldn't settle for a Nancy boy, and there's no denying Troy's a man's man.'

With a grudging, 'Yes, alright,' John steered them toward the bar. 'Now, I need a drink before undertaking my father of the bride duties.' Glancing dubiously at the stacked shelves behind the polished wood bar he muttered, 'I hope they serve Johnny Walker Blue here, at least.'

On seeing his smiling brother and sister-in-law approaching from down the corridor, Wolf's nervous, clean-shaven face split in a broad grin and he stepped forward to meet them. After giving Jake's extended hand a vigorous shake and surprising Amber with a quick hug, he escorted them to the bar. As they were introduced to the other wedding guests Jake held his breath, only releasing it when he heard Wolf get his wife's name right.

Punching his brother good-naturedly on a firm, suit-coated arm, Jake leaned in to say, 'Finally,' and was rewarded with a wry grin.

When he glimpsed more guests arriving, Wolf said apologetically, 'I'll have to catch up with you later, bro,' as he strode back to his post by the door.

Turning, Jake saw an elderly man walk up to them.

'You must be Wolf's brother, Jake,' the man said amiably, shaking Jake's hand. 'I'm Richard Salt, but you can call me Salty, everyone else does.' He beamed, white teeth bright against the tanned skin of his weather-beaten face. Tilting his head at the smiling woman by his side, he tapped the small hand resting on his forearm. 'And this lovely lady is Hannah Bourne, the bride's aunt.'

The couples exchanged pleasantries and then Salty turned to eye Jake. 'You're the best man I hear.'

'So they tell me.' Jake smiled and fingered his tie as a yell of, 'Hey, Jake!' reached his ears. Looking over, he saw two smartly dressed men charging toward him, and grinned.

'How're ya doin', buddy?' Bugs exclaimed, clapping him on the back. 'Long time no see.'

'I'm good, Bugs, real good.'

Jake's hand was firmly pumped and then Spooky stepped up and pumped it again.

'G'day mate. Good to see ya, and in such happy circumstances.'

All three swept a glance around the room which was steadily filling with jovial occupants.

Jake nodded. 'Yeah, real happy.' He threw his wife a wink and said, 'Amber and I never thought we'd see the day, to be honest.'

'Hah! Neither did we, mate, neither did we!' Slapping him on the shoulder again, Bugs announced,

'C'mon, my shout.' Turning to Salty he said fondly, 'You too, old fella.'

As their men were dragged to the bar, Amber and Hannah exchanged indulgent glances. 'Don't worry,' Hannah said, patting the younger woman's hand, 'Richard will be back with drinks for us. Let's find ourselves some seats and have a nice chat. We're family now, so we need to get to know each other.'

With all the expected guests assembled, the celebrant positioned Wolf and Jake in front of her before stepping up to the mic. She tapped sharply on a half-full champagne flute, then again, and again, until finally the noise died down. When she announced the ceremony was about to commence, the guests made their way to their seats, and all eyes turned expectantly toward the door.

Hearing a communal intake of breath, Wolf turned to see a vision in white at the end of the corridor. His mouth dropped open as he watched the bride – *his* bride – serenely making her way toward him, one slender hand linked through a regal John Modeen's tuxedo-clad arm. The simplicity of her floor-length, figure-hugging sheath in heavy ivory satin was softened by a delicately laced plunge back and drop-shoulder sleeves, and matched by a simple cluster of white and blush-pink rosebuds in her gleaming hair. In one hand she carried a beribboned bouquet of white and pink roses.

And nothing, not her stunning figure in the gorgeous dress, nor the picture-perfect blooms in her hair and bouquet, could outshine the glow on Modeen's face.

A proud John Modeen escorted his daughter down the aisle and stopped, to pass her hand into Wolf's, before stepping back to join Freda in the front row of chairs.

Wolf was oblivious to everything else but the woman by his side. He gazed down at her, spellbound, as they exchanged vows and rings, only managing to hold back until the celebrant introduced them as Mr and Mrs Troy Wolverton. Then, drawing her close, he bent his dark head and pressed a kiss on his wife's smiling lips, to loud applause and wolf-whistles. He only lifted his head again when Bugs yelled, 'Enough already! Get a room!' and laughter erupted.

Celebrations continued well into the night.

Bugs slapped Spooky on the back and sat down beside him. They sipped their beers, watching the newlyweds being congratulated, having photos taken, cutting the cake, dancing the wedding waltz under the glitzy disco ball – all the usual marital traditions.

Toward the end of the night, Ben and Emily were among the first to leave.

With a final kiss for Modeen and Wolf, Emily said

regretfully, 'It's been wonderful, and we'd love to stay on but our babysitter can't spend the night.'

Modeen took her hand and smiled warmly at her. 'Of course. Thanks so much for coming.'

Slapping Wolf on a broad shoulder, Ben said gruffly, 'Well done, mate. You've scored yourself a good one there.' He grinned. 'But you knew that already.' As they made to leave he leaned in to drop a kiss on Modeen's cheek and murmured, 'Don't forget to call me next week.'

Behind them, Salty twirled Hannah close by Bugs' and Spooky's table and put her into a dip. As her head fell back she gave the two men an upside-down smile and a wave.

Laughing, they saluted her and then Bugs turned to Spooky with a wry grin. 'When d'ya reckon it'll be our turn?'

Spooky was watching the couple twirl away. 'I'm sure Hannah will be up for another dance when Salty's had enough.'

Bugs rolled his eyes. 'No, I mean when do you think we'll settle down.'

Spooky gave a teasing grin. 'I knew what you meant, but ... who knows?' He shrugged and added pensively, 'Wasn't something I thought about when we were in the force, and now....' His brow creased. 'Maybe it's still not a good idea.'

'I know what y'mean. My first attempt didn't end well.' Bugs sighed and drained his beer glass. As they watched Modeen laughing up at Wolf when he put her in an extended dip on the dance floor, Bugs nudged Spooky. 'You don't think it's worth the risk to have what they've got?'

'Maybe, but we both saw the trouble they had when they left the agency.'

Bugs gave a thoughtful grunt as he watched Wolf pull Modeen close again. After a bit he said, 'You enjoy that stint workin' in the lab?' At Spooky's nod, he went on. 'Maybe you could secure a permanent job like that, and then think about settlin' down.'

'Yeah … maybe. I *did* enjoy the work.' Spooky's eyes took on a faraway look. 'Must admit, it would've been interesting to see what they eventually fitted that prototype into.'

———

At Mach 0.5, a US Air Force F-35A Lightning II multi-role fighter jet rocketed through the Aleutian mountains behind Ivanof Bay in Alaska's South West peninsula. As pilot Rick 'Raven' Sorenson wove his jet through the valley, warning alarms rang out in the cockpit. Gritting his teeth, Sorenson set off flares and manoeuvred the plane closer to the mountains.

When a Russian Vympel R-27 air-to-air missile exploded behind him, he grimaced and depressed a button on the throttle lever. 'Eielson Base,' he barked, 'this is Raven. Request *immediate* back-up. I have three hostile Terminators on my six, closing fast … I'm in deep shit.'

'Raven, this is Eielson Base.' The urgency in the operator's voice almost matched Sorenson's. 'Two F-18s have been scrambled, ETA ten minutes.'

With perspiration beading on his brow, Sorenson pushed the throttle full forward and barrel-rolled through a narrow canyon, growling through clenched teeth, 'Ten minutes … I'm not gonna last five.'

Concentrating on keeping his plane close – but not too close – to the mountains, Sorenson glanced at the heads-up display and took a double take. One of the three attacking planes had disappeared off the radar. It was there a second ago … where had it gone?

Then a new voice came over the comms. 'Raven, this is Wraith One. I've got your six.'

In the Russians' fractured attacking formation, the rear pilot in an SU-37 Terminator, stared in disbelief at the empty air where his wingman should've been. His eyes widened further as an F-22 Raptor nosed in as if completing the arrowhead formation.

Having eliminated one of the Terminators with a single burst from the pulse laser fitted to his F-22, Lieutenant Josh 'Voodoo' McMillan glanced at the other SU-37 beside him, and grinned.

This is just too easy.

As the SU-37 hastily peeled off to put distance

between them, McMillan ran his eyes over the sleek, aggressive-looking fighter. The Terminator had the advantage of size, he conceded, and carried an impressive arsenal. Then he focused his gaze on the remaining Vympel missile suspended from its wing, and his helmet-mounted cueing display followed his eye movements. When a second pulse from the Raptor ignited the charge in the missile's mid-section, the Terminator's pilot reached for the ejector seat handle just as his plane exploded in a blaze of fire.

McMillan had already changed his focus and was now hot on the tail of the remaining jet.

In the F-35A, Sorenson saw another dot disappear from the radar, and when the blip of the remaining jet banked left to cease its pursuit, he blew a sigh of relief through tightly pursed lips.

Recognising the lead fighter jet as a fifth generation Sukhoi T-50 PAK FA, McMillan followed as it went vertical, noting with satisfaction that this was the first time the two aircraft had been in such close proximity.

Muttering to himself, 'What's on your mind, Ivan? You gonna run or stay 'n fight?' he watched the Russian pilot put the Sukhoi into a vertical spin, and gave a grim smile. 'You tryin' for a visual on what took out your two comrades, buddy?'

At the top of the climb, the T-50 executed an inverted roll-over to dive back toward the mountains. Sticking close to the Russian's belly, the Raptor mirrored his manoeuvre and followed him down. Skilfully employing its thrust vectoring nozzles, the Sukhoi twisted and barrel-rolled tightly through the valley trying unsuccessfully to shake the F-22. When the valley branched around a mountain, the Sukhoi banked left as if admitting defeat.

Murmuring, 'You live to fight another day, Ivan,' McMillan banked the Raptor to the right, ending the pursuit. Flying low along the mountain range, he picked up Sorenson on radar and set a course to intercept him, only to see the T-50 coming up fast on the other side of the mountain range to his left.

Re-engaging.

Shaking his head and muttering, 'Bad idea, Ivan. Bad idea,' McMillan hit the brakes just before a gap in the mountains. As the Russian flew through the gap, McMillan fired the pulse laser, and the Sukhoi disintegrated across the valley.

In the F-35A, McMillan's voice came over the comms. 'Raven, this is Wraith One. All enemy aircraft are down.'

'Wraith One, identify.' Sorenson eased back the throttle and banked the Lightning around.

'Raven, this is Voodoo.'

'Where did you come from, Voodoo?'

'Took off from Eareckson air station on Shemya island and tracked the three bogies as they crossed the Bering Sea. Was movin' in to ID and intercept them when I heard your distress call.'

'I didn't pick up any missiles … what the hell did you take 'em out with?'

There was a pause and then McMillan's voice came back on. 'That's a story for another time, buddy.'

'Well I owe you one, Voodoo, thank you.'

'You're welcome Raven, and the name's Josh.'

'Rick.' Seeing the F-22 draw alongside his Lightning, Sorenson ran his eyes over the fighter. Bigger all round, and powered by two Pratt and Whitney thrust-vectoring turbofans, it looked every bit the Lightning's big brother.

In the Raptor's cockpit, McMillan picked up the fast-approaching Super Hornets on his radar. 'Looks like your escort is here, Rick, so I'll head back to Shemya.' Lining up his fighter so he could eyeball Sorenson, he gave a salute which was immediately returned. With an amiable, 'Catch ya in the blue another day, buddy,' he peeled off, put the Raptor into a victory roll and rocketed back to base.

———

If you've enjoyed **Modeen Redemption,** *I hope you'll consider posting a reivew on your retailer's site and/or on Goodreads. And don't miss Modeen's next thrilling adventures in the following instalments.*

FHJ

FROM NATSEC FILES

Name: Josephine Dakota MODEEN, known as "Modeen", "Jo", or "JD"

NatSec Alias: Josephine BENNET

Parents: John and Freda MODEEN

Spouse: Troy Wolverton, NatSec agent (alias Troy Ryan)

Children: Nil **Siblings:** Nil

DOB: 09/05/1986

Height: 5'11"

Hair: Platinum blonde, cropped short

Eyes: China blue

Character: Tough, clever, street-smart, courageous and decisive; has quick reflexes; can appear cool and aloof

Appearance: Tall, athletic, dresses boyishly but can be ultra-feminine when she chooses; has a strong but pretty face with fine features; normally wears a serious, self-possessed expression; has a scar on one cheek from a glancing bullet, and a deep scar on her left shoulder from a bullet that passed through the soft tissue

Private transport: Midnight blue Kawasaki GTR 1400cc motorbike

Weapon/s of choice: Walther PPX .9mm (referred to as "Walt")

Jobs: Soldier Regular Army; SASR specialist signaller and recipient of Medal of Gallantry and various service medals; Security Guard; NatSec Agent – Beta Team

Status: REACTIVATED

PRAISE FOR FRANK H JORDAN

'Holy Butt Kickers Batman! Frank Jordan can write a wicked story that mixes humor, adventure, and intrigue woven into a realistic plot. His characters are gritty and tough as nails. Love the accents and the people of Oz.'

— US REVIEWER

… [Jordan has] created a match for the baddies in Jo Modeen, a kick-ass heroine with nerves of steel and a size 9 boot….'

— THE CAIRNS POST NEWSPAPER

'There ain't nuthin' [sic] to dislike about Jo Modeen. Would love to [have] had her on our team back in Cambodia and Laos!'

— REVIEWER JR LEE

OTHER BOOKS IN THE SERIES

THE MODEEN FACTOR

Introducing kick-butt heroine Jo Modeen
She's beautiful, noble … and deadly

Josephine Dakota Modeen, recipient of the Medal for Gallantry in Action and the first woman to be accepted into the elite SASR, finds life after the Army unfulfilling. When contacted by her old CO, she knows it's not a social call. Ben Logan VC MG doesn't 'do' social calls, at least not to the members of his old squad now living in the 'real' world. Hearing from Ben means a mission, no exceptions….

The books in this series are available in ebook, paperback, and in ebook box sets of three. The first three instalments are also available as audio books from selected retailers.

THE MODEEN TRANSFORMATION

The 2nd action-filled Modeen adventure

Australian security agencies are on alert in the lead-up
to the 2014 international G20 Summit being held in
Brisbane, Queensland. Although aware of an increase
in web activity on the summit site and into the
backgrounds of its attending diplomats, even NatSec
intel can't know what the terrorist group known as
'The Spear of Allah' is planning.
Something ex-SASR soldier and now NatSec agent, Jo
Modeen, is about to find out in a very personal way….

MODEEN: RULES OF ENGAGEMENT

The 7th thrilling instalment

Modeen and other members of her old squad find themselves defending honour and truth, after being subpoenaed to provide statements to a military inquiry into allegations of war crimes.

Did Ben and his Special Forces squad blatantly breach the ADF's Rules of Engagement while on deployment, or is something more sinister afoot?

MODEEN: FLASHPOINT

The 8th explosive adventure

When an LNG tanker is sunk in the Philippine Sea
north of Papua New Guinea, the spotlight falls on the
lucrative liquefied natural gas market. Believing an
international cartel to be responsible, and that
Australia's LNG plants could be at risk, the CIA tasks
NatSec with gathering on-site intel.
Modeen's team is deployed to discover the saboteurs'
identities, determine their next target, and find out just
how far they will go....

THE JO MODEEN BOX SET: BOOKS 7-9

Due for release on 1 January, 2021

In *Modeen: Rules of Engagement*, Modeen and team find themselves defending honour and truth … and Ben's past actions.

In *Modeen: Flashpoint*, the sinking of an LNG tanker north of Papua New Guinea sees Modeen and team deployed to uncover those responsible, and determine what - or who - is the next intended target.

In *Modeen: Strikeforce*, British SAS and US Night Stalkers are deployed to Afghanistan to rescue pilots captured by the ruthless Red Group. It's an impressive strikeforce, but will it be enough?

The third box set is available as an ebook from your favourite online retailer.

www.ingramcontent.com/pod-product-compliance
Lightning Source LLC
Chambersburg PA
CBHW050158120726
47903CB00002B/670